Carried Away

USA Today Bestselling Author
P. DANGELICO

Carried Away

Copyright © 2020 P. Dangelico
All rights reserved.
ISBN: 9798653960765
Published by P. Dangelico

All rights reserved. No part of this book may be reproduced or transmitted in any form, including electronic or mechanical, without written permission from the publisher, except in the case of brief quotations embodied in critical articles or reviews. This is a work of fiction. Names, characters, places, events, and incidents are either the product of the author's imagination or used in a fictitious manner. Any resemblance to actual persons, living or dead, or actual events is purely coincidental. This book is licensed for your personal enjoyment only. This book may not be re-sold or given away to other people. If you would like to share this book with another person, please purchase an additional copy for each person you share it with. Thank you for respecting the author's work.

Cover Design: NAJLA QAMBER, Najla Qamber Designs
Playlist on Spotify
www.pdangelico.com

Chapter One

THERE ARE A FEW UNIVERSAL truths that still hold true. Not many, mind you. But at least a handful. Like…we need to keep our oceans clean. Who would argue with that? No one sane. Firefighters aren't paid nearly enough for what they do. They run into fire y'all. The Rolling Stones > the Beatles. By a landslide. Daylight savings should be abolished. I dare you to change my mind.

And lastly, having a mad crush on your boss is a bad idea. That's a clear loser in everyone's estimation.

Even worse, that in a moment of lax morals, overconfidence in one's desirability, and some uncharacteristic heavy drinking at the company winter holiday party you somehow end up kissing said boss in the bathroom. Not my finest moment but I've been lusting after him for the better part of the last four years so you can't blame a girl.

At present, I find myself in said boss's office making myself small in the chair opposite his and trying to avoid eye contact for obvious reasons.

"I have to let you go," Ben says. That's his name—my boss at So-And-So Media Corp, a name I can't divulge due to the NDA all employees sign upon being hired.

My eyebrow notches up, but that's about it. Just one eyebrow bump. Because although the wording is curious, I must've misunderstood. Or not heard him correctly. He's not firing me. There isn't a single solitary chance of that happening.

First of all, it's only ten in the morning and I haven't had my second Monster drink yet—stuff doesn't get real for me until after that second injection of caffeine. Therefore, it is a legit possibility that my brain is misfiring in a million different directions and making me think I am being shit-canned by the man who I've had a nauseating schoolgirl crush on for as long as I've known him. The same man, mind you, whose every semi-complimentary word I've hung onto like it's an edict from the heavens while he does me the honor of ignoring the undoubtedly hangdog, mildly brain damaged looks I give him.

Second of all…he needs me. The man can't get through the day without shouting my name at least six times, and it's never in ecstasy.

Ben leans back in his office chair with his hands

neatly laced together on his trim midsection, his expression blank while my eyes wander behind him, to the bookcase filled with journalism awards and travel memorabilia. It's a tangible reminder that Ben isn't just the pretty face willing to do all kinds of nasty things to me in my daydreams, he's also a ridiculously talented journalist who's amassed experience and proven himself on more than one occasion.

And therein lies the problem. I worship Ben, and in turn, he rides me like a rented mule and not in the way I wish he would.

"Carrie?"

My attention shoots back to his impressive face. This is not an overstatement. Ben has bone structure that would turn most people, men and women alike, neon green with envy.

A thin straight nose, a razor sharp jawline, thick dark brows frame moss green eyes, and a perpetual shadow covers the bottom half of his face because it's always five o'clock in Ben's world. Add the ghost of British accent to this cornucopia of awesomeness and it's almost an overkill of sex appeal.

And it doesn't end there. Nope. Because the sum of those parts is so much greater.

I once saw a picture of Ben taken at the Tripoli airport as he fled near captured by an ISIS cell. He wore a safari jacket, aviators, and a beat up Yankees ball cap. It made me so hot I got cramps. Freaking cramps! I thought my uterus was going to explode right there and then in the middle of the day as I sat at my cubicle stuffing my face with a roast beef on rye sandwich.

"Did you hear me?" he continues, his face expressionless save for a slow measured blink.

This isn't at all like him—Ben's usually smoldering raw sexual energy—but it's been super awkward between us the last few months. Hence, I do what we both have done since the night of the kiss—I pretend it's not happening. Sometimes I manage to convince myself the kiss didn't happen either.

Catching myself staring at the lips in question, I look away. Who am I kidding? Nothing's going to erase that memory. Not the way I bumped my forehead against his chest as he was exiting the bathroom I was entering. Not the feeling as I laughed and rubbed my forehead where it had impacted his hard chest. Not the image of him smiling down at me. Or when he wrapped those long fingers around my wrist and pulled me inside.

Yeah, I'm not forgetting that anytime soon.

Less than a minute later, I was unexpectedly pinned against the back of the door with his tongue down my throat. I had to open my eyes to make sure I wasn't imagining it. That's never a good sign. If you ever feel inclined to open your eyes in the midst of making out with your hot boss, something's probably wrong.

Was it the best kiss ever? No.

Was it terrible? No.

It just didn't live up to the fantasy and the fantasy had been nothing short of spectacular for years. Then again I was drunk, so maybe my memory of it hasn't served me well. Which is why I've chalked it up to my bad and not his.

After a few minutes of sloppy kissing, Ben pulled away, looking disheveled and uncharacteristically unsure of himself. He ran his hands through his hair as he apologized in that charming British way of his (which could probably get him out of murder rap) and stormed out, leaving me there alone to wonder what the heck had happened.

But that was six weeks ago and this is now. And now, sitting on his throne of accomplishments, Ben looks very sure of himself. Less so of me. Regardless, I'm not hitting the panic button because he can't fire me even if he wants to. I'm his go-getter. The one in the office that never *ever* says no to him. I'm absolutely certain he can't fire me any more than he can do without his right hand.

Impatiently, I glance at the iPhone resting on my lap. A mountain of research is waiting for me on my laptop—a story I brought to Ben that I'm working on for him—and the deadline is hanging over my head.

"To lunch?" is the only reasonable assumption. "I don't have time today."

Once again, I'll probably spend the weekend working. Lunch isn't even an option. My job is basically all I have and I really don't mind it. This is what I've always wanted, after all. What I've been working towards since I graduated top of my class from Arizona State with a BA in Journalism. Well, not exactly *this*. Not the trips to the dry cleaners for Ben. Not the hunt for the gluten-free pizza for Ben. Not the late nights I've spent double checking another journalist's work because Ben asked me to when he/she was too lazy to follow up on he/she's own sources.

What I mean by *this is all I have* is that I have goals to achieve, awards to win, stories to tell, and slaving for Ben is going to help me accomplish all that. Having a personal life comes in at a distant second in level of importance.

He makes a face and for the first time since I've been summoned to his office doubt creeps in. It's Ben's constipated face. I know it well. The corners of his mouth are tight and slightly turned up, his brow furrowed. I've seen it countless times when he's dumping whatever it-girl of the moment he's lost interest in.

"No, umm…for good." His eyes shift away, to the screen of his desktop computer before he can even finish the last consonant. The same combo of vowels and consonants that are, at present, echoing in my head like a death knell.

I…am…being fired.

"Are you alright?" he says an undetermined amount of time later.

No. No, I am not alright. I'm as far from alright as I could possibly be. I want to scream right now. Instead, I shove it back down and work on measuring my breathing before I faint.

The bottom just fell out of my life. I can't afford to be unemployed. Not now. Probably not ever.

My gaze falls on the small coffee stain on the right thigh of my wrinkled pants and anger the likes of which I've rarely felt before rises to the surface. It's a perfect visual representation of my life: unnoticed and under appreciated. Had I known what was in store for me today I would've gone to the dry cleaners to pick up the clothes that had been there for weeks because I've been working overtime. I would've worn the Nars Inappropriate Red lipstick and my Chloe suit, the one my sister bought me for my birthday, the one that makes me look somewhat like a badass bitch. And I would've most definitely washed my hair.

Instead, I find myself getting fired in the same wrinkled Banana Republic grey pantsuit I've worn all week with my hair in a ponytail because dry shampoo can't actually perform miracles no matter what they tell you looking like your run-of-the-mill basic bitch.

A dry, nervous chuckle bursts out of me. "Why?"

As my mouth is forming that word, the answer hits me with crystal clarity. My mind conjures images of the bathroom kiss, and heat blankets my neck.

"Why what?"

"Why am I being fired?" I clarify over the grinding of my molars. Just because I'm willing to sacrifice everything for the greater good doesn't mean I'm about to roll over and play dead on command. I want to hear it said out loud that I'm being fired over a kiss.

He makes a confused face. "For starters"—his head bobs to the left—"it was the initial tweet."

Tweet? What tweet? Until it dawns on me, and my eyes falls shut as my insides knot.

"It wasn't even a full tweet," I mutter. "I only reposted my original article. It was more like a…a twit."

"The man had just died, Carrie. You didn't even wait twenty-four hours."

Okay, so maybe I shouldn't have tweeted the police report and mugshot, but if you don't want that to do the time don't do the crime.

"And I apologized—"

"After you doubled down."

"Because people were speaking about him like he was some kind of Demi-God."

"And to many people, he was," he fires back, the rising volume of his voice indicating he's losing patience with me.

An explanation is in order here. The one big story I broke, the one that earned me the job as Ben's bitch, for lack of a better term, was a story I broke fresh out of school.

A famous NFL quarterback was rumored to have beaten his girlfriend so badly she sustained serious injuries. Single handedly, I tracked her down, gained her trust, and got her permission to write her side of the story. Eventually, she turned over a video recording of the fight to me exclusively. Turns out, she'd been recording his visits since the first time he'd pushed her around. Crack reporting if I don't say so myself. I can still feel the adrenaline rush of chasing that lead.

At the time, the story was mostly buried. News outlets were playing wait-and-see. The story came as a shock to his millions of fans, many of which had a hard time believing it about their golden boy, and they didn't want to be caught having to issue a retraction and possibly alienating viewers.

All that changed when I published the story of his past behavior, including the video of how it all went down. The story went viral and plausible deniability was no longer an option. The video evidence explicitly showed Mr. NFL Superstar was neither set up, nor the victim of a woman seeking a fat settlement. He was an abuser.

In the end, he essentially got off. The case was dropped when the victim refused to testify. I never blamed her for taking the payout—coming out as a victim of abuse against a major celebrity usually ends with the victim being threatened and victimized further—but it was disappointing. The NFL benched him for a year. He paid fines. There was a lot of talk about changing the code of conduct. Sports analysts debated whether he'd be cut from the team and who would have the *courage* to pick him up. But ultimately, the team kept him on the roster and all was quickly forgiven and forgotten when they went on to win another Super Bowl.

That was four years ago. This weekend he was killed in a jet ski accident.

The news coverage was round the clock. Pundits and super fans kept going on and on about what a great man he was so I felt it necessary to even the scales a bit, to remind people he wasn't all that simply because he could throw a ball.

Have you ever been *ratioed* on Twitter? Yeah, it's not a nice thing to have happen. I received an avalanche of replies to my tweet, all of which were beyond vile and probably illegal in some states. The angry villagers came after me with pitchforks and knives. I just didn't expect Ben to join them.

"So we're all going to ignore his criminal history because he threw a ball really well?"

"He did a lot of good for the community, funded a

number of very successful charities—"

"He was an abuser."

"And he paid for that."

"Not nearly enough."

"Carrie—"

"Ben…" I plead in my most pathetic voice. "Ben, please…" Desperation is setting in. When Ben sets his mind to something, he can rarely be convinced to abandon his position. One of the reasons he's so good at his job. "You can't fire me for this. I was on my personal Twitter account on my *own* time."

"Carrie, not only can I—check your contract—but I have to." He points to the ceiling. "Order came from up above."

"God wants me fired?"

A fleeting smirk replaces his blank expression, then he shrugs. "In a sense."

After that, an awkward silence falls in which I'm not sure if I want to cry or commit workplace violence. Ben continues to stare back, trying to give nothing away, but it's all in his eyes. The distance makes my stomach roil. He's not coming to my rescue. He's really cutting me loose.

His chair slowly swivels right. Then left. And for the

first time since I walked into his office four years ago for my interview and nearly swooned at the mere sight of him, I want to rearrange his face to look less pretty.

I've taken one *or ten* for the team, forgone an actual life in pursuit of the story while Ben claimed all the credit. And for what? To be canceled at the first sign of trouble.

"I'm getting death threats," I tell him. And that's the truth. People are crazy about their sports heroes.

Sinking deeper in his office chair, he runs his fingers through his salted brown hair. "Yes, that's… unfortunate."

It doesn't look like he means it. In fact, it looks like he doesn't give two turds either way.

"Look"—he sighs tiredly. Like I'm an inconvenience he wants to be rid of as quickly as possible—"lay low for a while. We can revisit in a few months. Say…after the storm dies down."

This is what loyalty gets me. Discarded over a tweet, thrown away like yesterday's news for reporting the truth. My Nan always said never trust a good-looking man.

Ben picks up his Starbuck's take-out cup and brings it to his lips, lips that have covered mine, lips I used to fantasize about…lips I want to punch at the moment. It's then I recall—Ben's left handed.

Chapter Two

"Get out of the car…Get out of the car right now and get in there. Prostrate yourself at the altar of sisterly good will, and you won't have to set up house on skid row," I tell myself.

There are times in life where one must accept his or her fate. This is not one of those times.

I pause the banging of my forehead on the steering wheel of my ancient Jetta to glance at my sister's shiny new custom-built house. I don't have many options, but going back to New York with my tail tucked will definitely not be one of them. Which is why I find myself in Pacific Palisades, parked in my sister's hand-crafted cobblestone driveway for the last twenty minutes, psyching myself up to go inside.

The two week eviction notice I found in my mailbox this morning said it's long past time I paid her a visit. I've been out of work for a month and have officially run out of money. Time to flex my ovaries and get in there, throw myself at her perfectly pedicured feet, and beg her to let me stay in her she-shed for an undetermined amount of time.

There's no other option, and I've contemplated all of them. Unemployment barely covers my rent, and most of my friends are either married or in long term relationships. Asking them to let me stay for a week is one thing, but I can't be sure how long my situation is going to last. And let's be real, if one is to abuse someone's hospitality it ought to be family.

This is going to take a lot of swallowed pride—thus the apprehension.

Jackie is one of those people that does everything right. She's overachieved at everything she's ever set her mind to. Life for her is a straight line at a perfect forty-five-degree angle. No wobble in her trajectory. Not even a slight pause, let alone a stumble. She's the perfect daughter, a blue-ribbon show pony. While I'm…not.

That's not a bad thing though. Because I've essentially been left alone to screw up with impunity. And I have…case in point.

"What are you doing?"

The familiar male voice startles me into an audible screech. "Jesus…Charlie!"

My brother-in-law bends down to peer into the open

driver's side window of my jalopy. He's dressed in sweats and a faded UCLA Bruins t-shirt, hair mussed, his pale blue eyes laughing at me from behind thick-rimmed black eyeglasses. His lips curl into an insidious smirk as he takes a sip of what is, without a doubt, ethically sourced coffee.

"You scared the crap out of me, you creep."

"Says the woman sitting in my driveway, talking to herself for the past twenty minutes." Turning, Charlie walks back toward the house. "Are you coming?"

I either get in there or pop a tent on the corner of San Vincente and Bundy. Grabbing the bag of fresh bagels I bought for the occasion, I dutifully follow after him.

Inside, Jackie is at the kitchen table, stuffing her face with yogurt and granola. Her dark brown eyes peer up at me and do a quick and brutal assessment of my short denim overalls/white tank top/Princess Leia hair buns combo. My sister has strong opinions of what a professional woman should dress like and my preferred style, the Princess Leia hair buns and eclectic clothes ain't it.

"I come bearing gifts," I say flashing the goody bag and take a seat at the table opposite the two of them. "And the overalls are Helmut Lang FYI."

"So inappropriate *and* expensive," she says right out of the starting gate, nodding, "cool." Another spoonful of food gets shoveled into her mouth. "I said to Charlie 'Look, babe, a bum has appropriated our driveway,' and then I said 'Oh, never mind, it's just my baby sister.' Do you ever wash your car?"

She's one to talk. The show pony is wearing a coffee stained USC Law sweatshirt, pajama bottoms, and her black hair is haphazardly piled on top of her head which, frankly, looks unwashed.

"I'm conserving water," I say, shrugging her off. That's only half true. In my heart, I do try to conserve water. In reality, I don't have a nickel to spare for luxuries such as car washes.

Jackie rolls her eyes, her cheeks stuffed with food. And yet dirty hair and all, she still looks gorgeous. My sister is one of those people that looks beautiful under any circumstance. Like her beauty takes adversity as a personal challenge and rises to the occasion every time. Tears only make her eyes look bigger. The flu turns her into a willowy heroine from a 19th century novel.

Me? I get so much as a sniffle and end up looking like Kermit the frog. It's fucking annoying.

We're pretty much polar opposites. I love fashion,

Carried Away

and travel, and the thrill of the chase. Jackie loves order and routine. By 10 am on any given Sunday, my older sister—older by five years—typically has done an hour of hot yoga, showered, blown out her hair, applied her makeup flawlessly, and grocery shopped for the week. This hot mess that is my sister nowadays is out of the norm because she's four and half months pregnant, and she's already had two miscarriages.

"Zelda called," Jackie casually announces to the table even though there's nothing casual about the subject.

The abbreviated version of our sad family tale is that our mother walked out on our family when I was ten and Jackie was fifteen. She left our father for a woman and moved to New York City to "actualize herself." That's the bullshit she left in a letter on the kitchen counter while Jackie and I were at school and Dad was at the hardware store. More on that later. So, yeah, the subject of our mother is a touchy one.

"Did you speak to her?"

Jackie shakes her head, lost in thought. "I didn't pick up."

I have zero doubt that I do not want Zelda anywhere near me or my life whereas Jackie is more conflicted. "Are you going to?"

"Are you?" she answers back, leveling me with a pointed stare. She knows the answer to that. I haven't spoken to her in four years, since my college graduation when she showed up uninvited, and I don't plan to start now.

"How's my niece?" I ask while I grab a fresh raisin bagel and slap a blob of cream cheese on it. Time to get off this topic.

"Nephew," Charlie chimes in.

"Fine," Jackie replies tightly, casting a faraway gaze out the glass patio door. She's become increasingly superstitious about this pregnancy. I'm convinced she thinks that if she makes a big deal out of it, she'll lose the baby again. "What's going on with Ben?"

She's purposely changing the subject, but I let it slide. I'm about to hit her up for a substantial favor and need her to stay in a good mood for that purpose. For a moment, I toy with the idea of coming clean about getting fired and toss that aside quickly. I'm not ready to make my pitch yet and I get only one chance at this. My sister is an excellent trial lawyer. I am no match for her silver tongue and battle-ready wit.

"Nothing…I think he's dating an on-camera chick from KTLA."

It's only half true. I'm pretty sure he dumped her right before he dumped me.

"Told you not to wait." She shrugs. "It's 2020. In case you haven't noticed. Women can ask men out. Imagine if I'd waited for Charlie to get a clue." She scoffs as she reaches into the paper bag on the table for a bagel.

"It would've never happened," I say around a mouthful of mine.

Jackie glances lovingly at Charlie whose rapt attention is on his phone. Even with unwashed hair, by LA metrics, which is saying a lot, Jackie is a ten. Charlie…eh, he's a five on a good day.

And yet my sister swears she saw him in the campus library, staring at his computer and tugging on his hair, and knew he was the one.

"It would've never happened," my sister echoes back. "Right, babe? Remember when I threw myself at you?"

"All part of my master plan to make you fall in love with me," he deadpans, not once glancing up from whatever has captivated his attention on the phone.

"Well it worked," Jackie replies smugly, her cheeks puffed out with food, full lips the perfect shade of pink.

Looking up, my brother-in-law gives his wife a soft smile and leans closer for a brief kiss. Five years of marriage, two miscarriages, and they're still disgustingly in love. Personally, I've never experienced that elusive emotion, but one minute in their presence and it makes anyone a true believer.

"I got fired," hurls out of me while they're still basking in the glow of their good fortune. I'm terrible at keeping secrets. Probably one of the reasons I love reporting the news.

Two heads swivel to face me. Charlie's expression is carefully neutral, save for his blondish brownish eyebrows creeping up his forehead, while Jackie's is blank but emitting a decidedly unfriendly vibe.

"No," she says, her full lips forming the word slowly.

"All I need is a few weeks to get back on my f—"

"No."

This is the part where I explain that all those other times I needed a helping hand Jackie was the one to offer.

"Just hear me out—"

"No." She stuffs another piece of bagel in her mouth, head shaking rapidly. "What happened to your severance pay?"

"Bills..."

Jackie's eyes narrow to slits. "Who did you give it to this time?"

"Mrs. Nowicki's cat has feline leukemia and I couldn't *not* help."

Everyone has a bad habit, right? I sublet in a rent-controlled building and many of the other tenants have been there forever, most of which are north of seventy. Can I help it if I have a soft spot for old people? No, I can't.

"You don't even like cats," my sister barks back.

That's true. "But I do like Mrs. Nowicki." My attention moves to her right and I assume my most pitiful expression. "Charlie…"

"No," Jackie cuts in.

"Your meat puppet can speak for itself, Jacqueline."

"Hey…" Charlie responds with literally no emotional reaction. It's impossible to get Charlie to be anything less than absolutely chill.

"Two weeks. That's all I need."

Jackie chuckles sarcastically. "That's a lie and we both know it."

"Charlie…"

"Can't," he says while his eyes dart sideways to get a read on my sister.

"Why not? You have an entire she-shed"—I wave behind me to the backyard—"not serving any purpose."

"Because I like having sex with your sister—and we call it a pool house."

"Gross, dude. TMI." My attention shifts back to Jackie; Charlie seems to be a lost cause. "I could help around the house. I could help with…the cat." That sounds totally bogus to my own ears but what other choice do I have? She knows I'm a lousy cook and an even worse housekeeper.

"Like you helped when we went to Napa?" she responds without missing a beat. She's referring to an incident with Jackie's precious black Main Coon cat. My grandmother used to breeds these monsters and Elmo was the pick of the last litter she bred.

For the record, there's something seriously diabolical about that cat. The damn thing has the ability to steal your soul by simply looking at you. I'm fairly certain he screws with my head for kicks.

Bottom line, the freaking cat somehow snuck out, and I spent a day and a half making up a story of how a door-to-door salesman broke in and stole him. Elmo showed up a few hours after Jackie and Charlie got home, basically giving me the finger, and my sister didn't murder me. See? Happy ending.

"Elmo hates me. He was planning to kill me in my

sleep."

"Elmo is a cat. He doesn't have the ability to plan—"

"Says you. I found him standing over me in the middle of the night, ready to smother me with a pillow."

"If he wanted to smother you, he would've sat on your face."

Elmo is as big as my car. She's not exaggerating. "Please. I'm begging you. This is the last time."

"That's what you said last time and the time before that."

"What are big sisters for, right?"

"For knowing when to say *no*. You need to go home and get your shit together. Dad needs someone to help out—Maggie is retiring. Did he tell you?" Maggie is the assistant manager of Comfort Cottages, my Dad's hotel in the Adirondack Mountains in New York.

He might have, and I missed it.

Jackie shrugs, expression completely void of any sympathy. "It's perfect timing."

Yeah, no. No, it isn't perfect at all. I hate the cold. I hate it with the burning heat of a thousand erupting volcanoes, one of the many reasons I'm happy to call Los Angeles home. My head is shaking before she utters the last vowel. "Lake Placid? Hell no."

"Yes."

She can't mean it. "No, Jackie, please. I can't go back there." For so, so, so many reasons. My childhood was not a happy time in my life. Let's just leave it at that.

Steely resolve shoots out of her big brown eyes and my stomach drops. Crap. That's her courtroom look. I'd have a better chance of moving a mountain than change her mind.

"It's too cold. You know I can't handle the cold."

"Dad needs help. Nan can't move around like she used to. It'll be good for you and them."

She means it. I am quietly devastated. The food I just consumed sits like a ball of lead in my gut, making me queasy.

"You're really not going to let me stay here?" It never even crossed my mind that she would refuse to help. Jackie is the one I've always been able to count on to come through for me.

"I'm going to do something even better for you—I'm going to let you figure it out for yourself."

An eerie silence takes over the room. I haven't been home since I left for college eight years ago. Dad and Nan come out to LA every other year, so it hasn't been an issue.

I've been dreading this day, even though I knew it was coming. Except I wanted to return the hero, hoisting trophies above my head. Metaphorically speaking, of course. Instead, I have to drag my sorry ass home unemployed and broke. This is not how I saw my life going.

"Fine. But I get to borrow your cold weather wardrobe," I mutter, resigned to the abject humiliation I'm bound to face. Jackie has a killer wardrobe. If I'm going to get dragged in real life, I'd like to do it in style.

"One coat," my sister, the master negotiator, counters.

"The Ralph Lauren Navajo coat."

"Get real. No, absolutely not that one."

"We'll see."

Chapter Three

"Did I get you with my elbow?" says the guy seated to my right in the aisle seat. Yes, he did as a matter of fact, for the third time as he adjusted his noise canceling headphones.

"That's okay," I answer, shrinking even more into my middle seat.

Let me tell you what hell looks like. In fact, let me tell you what hell looks, smells, and sounds like. Hell is the second to last row on a late flight from O'Hare to Albany sitting next to an oversized overweight giant who smells like a combination of sautéed onions, feet, and low rent booze, who breathes so loudly it almost drowns out the engines roaring next to my head, and not being able to recline and read because an angry six-year-old keeps kicking the back of my seat while he screams, "I want grilled cheese!"

The flight from hell lasts six and half hours due to two connecting stops. Six and a half hours of my life that I would like to permanently scrub from my memory. In

Carried Away

general, I'm a good sport about stuff like this. As a journalist, roughing it is part of the job description. No, I haven't exactly skipped through the war-torn streets of Idlib yet, but I've slept in my junker in pursuit of a story on more than a few occasions. And I've ventured into places that most people with a modicum of self-preservation would never step foot into.

That said, heading back to Lake Placid for an undetermined amount of time has me raw to the bone and feeling not at all forgiving of my liberties being infringed.

It's not like my loathing of my hometown is baseless. I have my reasons. Lake Placid is trapped in a time warp for me. Everything about it triggers all the awful feelings that I've worked hard to leave behind. Which is why I don't allow myself to think about it for more than a nanosecond. When I left for college, that part of my life died, and I'd like for it to stay that way.

Almost on cue, the number one reason for all my problems appears on the small TV screen embedded in the seat before me. God has a sick sense of humor.

CNN is on and the volume is off, but Dr. Zelda Anderson is flapping her lips and smiling at Chris Cuomo like she's planning to eat him alive. And that's not hyperbole; the woman is a super-predator. My mother is one of those celebrity therapist that writes books and makes TV appearances. I'm pretty sure she's never had any legit patients that she's cared for because that would require the ability to empathize. No, Zelda is content with spouting words of wisdom she doesn't live by and getting her hair and makeup done.

I can't press the button fast enough, and heave a sigh of relief when the screen goes dark.

The plane ride from hell ends around 10 pm with a bumpy landing and a kick to the back of my seat hard enough to displace the last vertebra of my spine. This happens seconds from me standing and screaming, "Will somebody get this child a fucking grilled cheese!"

The bone-jarring landing is followed up by a foot race to the car rental counters when we're informed by loudspeaker that all connecting flights are canceled due to the mother-of-all-storms gathering along the East coast. With two large and overstuffed suitcases dragging behind me, running fast is a relative term.

When I finally get there, I'm the umpteenth person in line. I pull out my phone while I wait and check my Twitter feed. 1,038 new alerts to my tweet, which I refuse to delete out of principal.

Carried Away

Most of them are suggesting I do things to the orifices of my body that would end my life. One threatens to doxx me. For those of you unfamiliar with this practice, it means to post personal information like an address of where you live and work online for public consumption, quite possibly putting someone in harm's way.

For the first time since I was fired, I'm grateful that I'm homeless and unemployed.

Turning off my phone, I shove it in the back pocket of my jeans. An excruciating half an hour later, it's finally my turn. The woman working the car rental desk looks ready to quit. Late sixties, judging by the frizzy cloud of gray hair and slight hang of her jowls. The name tag on her red long sleeve polo shirt reads, Delores.

Delores is not a happy camper. Her thin lips are pinched, accenting the smoker's lines around them, and she has the vacant stare of a person who has dealt with way too much BS for one day. Whoever came before me has obviously given this poor woman a hard time so I decide to kill Delores with kindness and slap a smile on my face. It always pays to be kind.

"Hi. Hello, Delores. I need a car, the cheapest you've got please."

No surprise, Delores is not charmed by my forced

cheerfulness. She sighs tiredly and looks down at her computer screen. "Don't have much left. And I should warn ya, storm's coming. You won't get far."

My temper is on a hair trigger and it comes up quickly. It's close to midnight, I haven't eaten anything outside of a free bag of potato chips in ten hours, and I know I have a two-and-a-half-hour drive ahead of me. A debate is not what I'm looking for right now.

"I'll take my chances," I tell her, my perkiness and fake smile fading along with my patience.

"They're sayin' a nor'easter—a bad one."

My smile drops like a brick. "Duly noted. Can I get a car please?" I shove my driver's license and credit card at her in the hopes she'll stop giving me the weather report and start printing the rental contract.

But Delores is not deterred. Oh, no. She adds a disapproving head shake to her repertoire and presses on. "With a bomb cyclone."

"Look—" I start, taking a deep breath to bank my frustration. "Delores, right? I'm not some showboating tourist, okay? I grew up around here. A few feet of snow are a walk in the park for me. We're good, alright?"

Delores and the patronizing look on her face are turning out to be more annoying than the grilled cheese kid.

"We got one econ rental left. It won't be good in the snow, but it's all we got."

A smile of pure unadulterated triumph breaks across my face. "I'll take it," I nearly shout, close to double-fist pumping the air.

She hands me the rental contract on which is written…Nissan Cube. I glance up into Delores's determined expression and it tells me that if I say one word, that precious Cube is no longer mine. Needless to say, I'm not taking any chances of getting stuck in Albany with my almost maxed out credit cards. I mumble a thanks, and ten minutes later I am hustling out to the underground parking garage dragging two large suitcases behind me to claim my bright orange Nissan Cube.

As I pull the Cube out of the underground garage, snowflakes fall gently on the windshield. It seems everyone is watching the same weather report because the streets of Albany are nearly deserted. The light from the street lamps catch the snow, the night alight with a romantic glow as I navigate the backroads to the thruway. There's something magical about softly falling snow and a tickle of hope stirs in my chest. Or maybe it's wishful thinking. It's in my nature to be positive.

Life is a journey someone much wiser than me once said. And if that's true, then maybe mine is destined to have few more twists and turns than most.

Every Day Is A Winding Road by Sheryl Crow comes on the radio. I turn up the volume, breathing a sigh of relief that for now the worst is behind me. And as the orange Cube chugs up the thruway, I sing along. Who the hell knows, maybe Sheryl is onto something.

* * *

The worst is most definitely *not* behind me. In fact, it's on me, over me, and under me. I'll be picking it out of my teeth and underwear soon. Half an hour into my trip, I am getting creamed by the worst.

Let me just say this, a bomb cyclone is not something to trifle with. Officially, I am a showboating tourist. I am a trash-talking, know-it-all, showboating tourist. This is not the first time my mouth has gotten me into trouble—no surprise there—but it has never put my life in actual jeopardy before.

I don't remember snowfall like this. Even though it has technically been eight years since I've lived here; I don't remember anything like this at all. And here's more bad news—it's getting progressively worse the farther north of Albany I drive.

A two-hour trip turns into a hair-raising, anxiety-inducing four-and-a-half hour one, most of which is conducted in near whiteout conditions with me bent over the steering wheel, clutching it like it's the last roll of toilet paper during a worldwide pandemic. The entire way I'm talking to the car. It's all I can do to keep the nervous breakdown at bay.

"What a good girl you are. So handy and brave… Look at you, defying the odds…They said she couldn't do it, but she persisted…"

Only by the grace of God do I somehow make the turn onto 73 west headed toward downtown Lake Placid. It feels like a race with time; the closer I get to my destination the more brutal the conditions get.

Inching my way down the two-lane highway, the snow banked up the sides gets higher and higher until it closes in around me and I can't see the road anymore.

That's when all hell breaks loose.

It happens very fast and simultaneously very slowly—like I'm stuck in a bad *Fast And Furious* take. The little orange car that can just can't do it anymore. As my heart pounds with fuel-injected fear, the Cube starts fishtailing, the back wheels spinning and spinning. I freeze, unconsciously holding my breath, because doing anything else is beyond my pay grade.

This is where my luck ends. I never had much to begin with, but right here and now the little I do have peters out. The scream is stuck in my throat as the car slides sideways off the street, crashes through a pile of snow, and eventually into a cluster of pine trees. The driver's side door slams into an unmovable object, and I slam my head into the driver's side window.

Once the world stops spinning, I take a minute to assess the damage. Other than my throbbing brain, which I try and fail to soothe by rubbing, I'm alive and in one piece, seemingly unscathed for now. I say seemingly because it's then I realize that I'm way off road, hidden from any vehicles passing, and the snow is coming down fast with flakes the size of frisbees. It'll be mere seconds before the entire car is covered. The windshield wipers, working hard to clear the blanket of falling snow, just can't keep up with the onslaught, and before long I'm sitting in a tin igloo—or a casket. Whichever.

I turn off the engine. The exhaust pipe could be blocked (who knew all the true crime documentaries I've binged would come in handy) and dying softly from co2 poisoning is not my preferred choice…not that I have a choice. The thought turns my stomach. I still have a ton of life to live. This is not how my story ends.

The temperature inside the car quickly plummets, and since I'm not a complete idiot, I decide the best course of action is to put on as many clothes as possible. Crawling out of the driver's seat, I get in the back and start opening the suitcases, which is no easy task when I'm shaking, and my fingers are numb. Teeth chattering, I strip off my sister's Canada Goose maxi coat and start piling on sweaters, undershirts—anything that I can cram on gets crammed on because it is flipping cold.

"I can't die here. This is not how my story ends. Hell no. I *refuse* to die like Jack Nicholson in *The Shining*."

Once I get all the clothes on, I lie down in the back, clutching my phone. Going out in this storm would be utter madness and I'm not desperate enough yet. I've got a large water bottle and a pack of strawberry Twizzlers to hold me over for the night. Besides, Nicholson's frozen face keeps flashing before my eyes. No, the best course of action is to hunker down until the storm abates. After that, I'll venture forth and see if I can flag down a state snowplow. This is a major road in and out of town; they won't wait long to clear it.

The phone battery icon blinks green. It's fully

charged. And I have an extra battery with me. Little good that does me with a nonexistent signal, but at least I'm not one of those people on the evening news that finds themselves in dire straits with no battery juice.

The quote running in the byline flashes before my eyes. *"Yeah, she died. But at least she had a fully charged phone and a back-up battery."*

That doesn't sound great either.

Save for the dim light of my screen, the cab is dark and it's getting colder by the second. My focus is waning, and the courage I've marshaled begins to slowly seep out of me. All that is left in its wake is a deep fear that I am good and truly screwed and I can't talk myself out of it like I usually do. Trying to swallow the fear that balls in my throat only helps to drive it to the surface.

You know that *oh shit* moment? The one that inevitably everyone has at least once in his or her life. Like *oh, shit, I shouldn't have applied self-tanner the night before my big job interview.* Or, *oh shit, all that cheese and champagne at the big fancy New Year's Eve party was a bad idea.* Or *oh shit, did I just send that pic of the suspicious beauty mark on my boob to everyone on my contact list instead of to my sister?* Yeah, well, this is definitely my *oh shit* moment.

Even beneath the mountain of clothes I'm buried under, my body is shaking violently, my anxiety slowly climbing until I'm on the verge of tears. That's when the thoughts sneak in. The bad ones. There's so much I haven't done. So much I haven't seen. Too much I haven't accomplished yet. I'm usually really good at getting myself out of trouble, but there is a very real chance I may not come out ahead this time and all those boxes I haven't checked yet taunt me. What the hell have I been doing with my time?

"God, if you're listening, I have a list…you there, buddy?" Fuck, I feel alone. My vision gets blurry as tears pool in the corner of my eyes. "Okay, here it is if you're interested…I would like to meet my niece or nephew. You can't deny me that." The thought of never seeing Jackie again has me crying so hard my eyes hurt, and it's so cold the tears sting. "Also, I would like to fall in love just once…and Ben doesn't count. Fucking hell, this is not how my story ends! Sorry, I apologize for the salty language but I'm cold and you know how much I hate the cold…"

I can't die like this, frozen, in the middle of nowhere, unemployed and broke.

"A Pulitzer would be nice. I'm not saying it's a must,

more like a wish if you're in a generous mood tonight."

It's so dark that if I wasn't exhausted from shaking I would be hyperventilating. As it stands my lungs burn from the frigid air. Shallow breaths are all I can tolerate. My eyelids feel like they weigh a hundred pounds. I'm tired, so tired of shaking, of feeling cold and anxious, of thinking about all the things I'll miss out on.

I send my father and Nan a mental *I love you*. I tell Jackie that she's the best big sister ever, even if it's that bitch's fault that I'm in this mess. Then I tell her I don't want her to blame herself.

And the last thought that stays with me as I drift away. Not something deep and meaningful, nothing noble. All I can think is…fucking Delores was right.

* * *

The sound of scratching wakes me from a perfectly good dream in which I'm a human popsicle and Ben is licking me. It annoys me; that I'm being awoken. It's the only thing giving me relief from the pain in my head and the cold making my skin simultaneously hypersensitive and numb.

My eyes slowly blink open to an endless void. I can't see a thing. Which means I'm deceased—or on my way there. It certainly seems like it. I'm no longer shaking, and my body is dead weight. I don't even try to move because I'm afraid I won't be able to.

The noise gets louder.

Someone is outside the car, I surmise with what little ability to think straight I still possess. Suddenly, the windows on the side of the car I'm facing clear of snow and I can make out the faint outline of a person. By the looks of it, it's a him and he's large. The big guy is moving his arms and hands back and forth, quickly clearing snow off the Cube as more falls at an alarming rate.

This is interesting, I think to myself. I wonder what happens next. That's about it though. I'm too tired to care or hold a thought in my head for longer than a second. It's more an amusing distraction, an action movie I'm watching from afar.

The man furiously working to clear the snow looks to be wrapped in a rainbow flag. Huh, that's interesting. With snow clinging to his head and beard, he reminds me of Santa. Also very interesting.

Big gay Santa's got a really harsh look on his face, his brow furrowed deeply as he works. Maybe it's more horror movie than action. If he says, *"Here's Johnny,"* when he finally gets the door open, I'll know I'm officially dead.

Gay Santa gets aggressive with the Cube and the car starts rocking. He seems to be upset that he can't get the door open, and I'm no help. I can't move. It's just too much of an effort to pick up my head. Reaching over to hit the Unlock button would require a crane and I don't have one handy right now. I'm rooting for him, though. Somewhere in the detached part of my brain that has split from reality, I hope he saves me. Mentally and morally, big gay Santa has all my support.

That's when things escalate. He stops pulling on the door long enough to draw back his elbow and crash it into the window. It shatters loudly. Good thing I'm dead because I can't afford to pay for that.

"Hey! Hey, you awake?" he says poking his big white head in the dark cab. His voice is raspy. Not your typical rasp, like when your throat is dry. That's not what this is. This guy sounds like he gargles with broken glass and battery acid on the regular. Weird that I would think that while I'm deceased but this is where we're at.

"Ma'am? Are you hurt?"

What do you think? Is on the tip of my tongue but it comes out as, "yeahlittleIdon'tknow."

"I'm comin' to get you."

Reaching in, he unlocks the back door and pulls and pulls until it creaks open halfway. Then the unpleasant part. A very bright light shines in my face, forcing me to slam my eyes shut.

"Nahhoooo," I hear myself cry out. The light hurts my head something fierce. I bury my face in the clothes I have piled over me. The sound of gay Santa sucking in a breath has me wondering what the drama is about.

"I'm getting you out. Just…gimme a minute."

The light disappears, and the pile of clothes on top of me is pushed off. I know this because I'm getting colder, which I didn't think was possible. Shortly after that, there's some ham-fisted jostling, and arms the size of tree trunks scoop under my knees and armpits.

Next thing I know, I'm ripped out the car with no warning. Falling snow covers my face, my closed eyes, clinging to my eyelashes. It's cold and annoying and makes me turtle into my jacket. I feel bruised and battered. I may not be dead yet, but I'm too tired to stay awake. Last thing I remember is gay Santa murmuring, "I've got you. You're safe now." Then, "I'm sorry."

I know I hit my head and I'm halfway to becoming a human popsicle, but he sounds drunk…or something.

Chapter Four

A BRIGHT LIGHT HITS MY eyelids. It might as well have pulled me out of the grave because I feel dead. Sore and in a bad mood, I crack open my eyes slowly and at first the strange surroundings startle me. Until I reach up and feel the protruding lump and subsequent throb on the side of my head. Then I'm reminded of the prior night's events in high-definition.

I'm lying on a ratty oversized leather couch. It's not entirely uncomfortable, however, so that's good. And there's a goose down blanket over me and pillow under my head. The pillow smells strangely similar to the Moroccan Oil shampoo I use. Don't know why I notice that but I do.

I take stock of the room. This farmhouse looks ready to be condemned. The yellow 1950s wallpaper on the walls is peeling, water stains cover the high ceiling, and the fire place is in the late stages of decay; half the bricks are in a pile inside. As for the floor…gross. It's an ugly wall-to-wall green carpet, torn out in some areas, stained in others with what appears to be paint of every color. Sienna, magenta, cerulean blue, and lemon yellow. A veritable rainbow of drips and drabs of bright color.

I'm still wearing all the clothes I had on last night so it's a little hard to sit upright. And when I finally do manage it, by rolling onto my side and pushing myself up, I find the same colored stains on my sweater. Yikes.

My sister's pink cashmere sweater has a big splatter of blue oil-based paint over one nipple and a yellow one on the sleeve. Jackie is going to be pissed. Then again, serves her right for what she did to me.

Gingerly, I struggle to get my broken body off the couch. First thing first, I need to find the guy who saved my life. Gay Santa. It's all coming back to me now. The crash, his selfless act of bravery. There's no doubt Gay Santa is the only reason I'm alive right now.

Passing a window, I can see the conditions outside are still apocalyptic. It's snowing. And not just snowing; it's snowing sideways.

This is not romantic. At all. The only stirring this elicits is nausea, a hypersensitivity of the skin probably due to a mild case of frostbite, and a reminder that I hit my head. I take back every nice thing I ever said about snow.

The good news is that this hellhole is warmish. The fireplace is out of service but the heat is definitely still working. The rest of the news is all bad. No bars on my cellphone and I can't find my red Pumas anywhere. All that separates my bare skin from whatever died on this carpet is a pair of wool socks.

"Hello," I half whisper as I slowly creep through the house. I'm not feeling half as courageous this morning as I was last night. Yes, he's a big gay mountain man who saved my life, but I can't be sure what his intentions are. He could have saved me for nefarious purposes. What I *am* sure about is that I've seen *Motel Hell* one too many times as a kid and I'm not keen on becoming beef jerky.

"Hello?" I whisper louder and get no response. The only sound that answers back is the howling of the wind outside and the creaking of this old farmhouse, which for the record is beyond creepy. I'm barely holding onto my imagination as it tries to run away with me.

Wandering, I enter another large room with the door wide open. It must have been a family room as some point, but all that remains now is a beat-up recliner sitting in the middle, a small side table next to it, and a brand new 60-inch flat screen TV mounted on the wall with a hockey puck stuck in the middle of it. It's for moments like these that the phrase *stranger than fiction* was coined.

A sound alerts me that I am no longer alone. A snort of sorts. I walk around to the front of the recliner and discover gay Santa sleeping soundly. I clear my throat, hoping that's enough to wake him, and get nothing in return. Not a twitch, not a lifting of an eyelid. No wakey.

So I move closer, with only an arm's length separating us. It's the first time I get a good look at…my savior? Meh, too melodramatic. Good Samaritan? Yeah, that sounds a little more dignified.

Barely fitting in the chair, he's as big as I remember from the night before. His forearms bulge against the faded red thermal he's wearing. The sleeves pushed up to the elbows reveal a black tattoo branching up his arm. It's then I notice his shirt is covered in paint. So are his hands, loosely hanging off the arm rest. I can even see a streak of green on his forehead. As for the rest of him—well-defined trapezius muscles bridge the distance between his neck and shoulders. His biceps are thick but not bulky, and his forearms corded. Covered in grey sweatpants, his long legs hang past the foot rest.

His face makes a much better second impression. He's younger than I first thought. Maybe early thirties.

His hair is a deep rich brown and in need of a trim, his jaw is covered in a very short beard. His nose has seen better days; it looks like it's been broken a time or two judging by the bump on the bridge. But it's his eyes that get all the credit. His brows are dark slashes that end in an exaggerated natural arch, and his lashes are thick and spiky.

His face is too harsh to be pretty, but he has a certain appeal. I'm sure he drives the boys crazy in his own way. I mean, if you like that sort of thing—the alpha, he-man, gym rat type.

Which I don't.

I like men that can debate the merits and detriments of the European Union, sophisticated men who like to travel and share books, who know more about the world than I do. Ben, in other words, that motherfu—

Gay Santa snorts and repositions his head. This guy sleeps like the dead.

Time to wake the sleeping beast. I tap a very hard forearm with my index finger, then wait. "Umm, hey guy…hi…hello?"

No reaction, so I tap again. This time his face puckers, brow contorts, lips nearly disappear. If I met this face in a dark alley I would definitely run. Unless, or course, it was in the middle of the mother-of-all-snowstorms. In which case I would need him to save me before he turned into beef jerky.

Aside from the face scrunching business, good Samaritan doesn't budge. On the carpet next to the chair, my attention falls on a shiny object. An empty bottle of whiskey. Jesus, is he hung over? Leaning in, I sniff, sniff again. Definitely sauced. Which makes sense now. He said some strange things last night. I just happened to be too cold to care at the time.

"Hello. Hey there. Hiii."

The forced cheerfulness finally does the trick. His eyes crack open, focus on me with all the intensity of a sniper rifle, and wait.

Automatically, I reach up and touch my buns. I may be half dead, but I'm still a girl. No surprise, they're destroyed, hanging off my head. More limp biscuits than cinnamon buns. In addition, my eye makeup is undoubtedly down my face with all the crying, and my arms are sticking out to the side with all the clothes I have on. I must look a fright, but that works in my favor right now.

"Hi. Sorry to wake you but…hi, I'm Carrie Anderson, the woman you saved last night from, well, basically freezing to death. I can't thank you enough. Really, thank you. I don't know what I would've done if you hadn't found me...umm, I mean, except die. Anyway, do you have a landline? I don't have any bars on my phone." I hold up the phone as evidence, but he doesn't seem to be interested. His gaze hasn't left my face once since he cracked them open. Not to mention, his silence is starting to unnerve me.

It's then it dawns on me...he doesn't speak English. That's why he sounded strange last night. He was speaking in Spanish.

"Shoot...shoot. I'm sorry I don't speak Spanish. No speak Español." I make a face because it really is a travesty that after four years of living in Arizona and four more living in L.A. and listening to my Spanish For Dummies audio on my way to work, all I can say is, "Dónde está el baño."

"Do you understand? Phone? Telephone? I need to call people," I repeat with some deadass cringe pantomiming of a phone.

He blinks. "Turner."

Turner? What the heck does that mean? It doesn't even sound like Spanish. This is where Google translate would come in handy.

"I'm sorry, I don't understand," I reply, my exasperation coming through loud and clear. By the way he's staring at me, he must think I'm insane. "I can't believe the month I'm having! Make that the year. 2020 sucks!" I tip my head back, searching for guidance, a sign, anything.

The silence persists and my attention returns to big gay Spanish Santa. His brows draw down.

"I'm not mad at you. I'm sorry I'm shouting. I have a bad habit of talking to myself out loud…"

A habit I picked up during all the late nights I spent in an empty office doing research. As a way to quiet the fear of being there alone. Why I'm telling this guy is beyond me. "Dónde está telephono?" I whine one last time.

Sitting up, he stretches his neck side to side. Then, once again, he aims the full power of his attention at me, and I shrink back. Those dark blue eyes are very intense.

"Step aside please."

What the heck…what the heck. Burning shame crawls up my neck. "Oh, ha…uh, yeah, sorry."

I'm having a *really* bad month.

I scoot out of the way and he rises from the recliner in one fluid motion. Then he stretches. Arms to the ceiling, he bends left, then right, and his shirt tags along for the ride, revealing a happy trail and a set of grooves next to his hip bones only <u>comic book villains</u> and gym rats possess.

The shirt comes down and my eyes slowly climb over him. It's hard not to. This is when I get the full picture of how powerfully built he really is. His shoulders, his chest, his thighs. What's equally hard to miss is how powerless I am in comparison.

Despite that I'm no slouch at 5'6," I have zero muscle and even less desire to build any. I'd go so far as to say my thumb is my strongest appendage, clearly due to all the ill-advised tweets I like to send. Or maybe my tongue for obvious reasons. Either way, this guy could squash me with one hand if he wanted to. Let's hope he doesn't.

While I remain rooted to the floor trying to look as unappealing as possible, I catch him eyeballing me—measuring me up. It's a stealthy quick assessment, but I catch it anyway. I'm a pro at observation—wouldn't be very good at my job if I wasn't—and the disinterested act he's putting on isn't fooling anyone.

Not that I'm a great temptation or anything—I look like the Pillsbury dough boy right now—but if he wasn't gay, I'd be a little more concerned. All I can hope for is that he's not sizing me up for a skin suit.

His gaze drops and he walks out of the room without a word.

"Turner…" I scurry after him, out of the room. "Turner, right? That's your name?"

"Don't wear it out," he replies, his back retreating down the hall. He enters what one would hypothetically call a kitchen, but in reality looks more like a dungeon for butchering things. Fingers crossed it isn't people.

Slowly, I follow and stop at the threshold of the room. Physical distancing is my friend right now. I don't know who this guy is or what he's really capable of and I will not be the dumb girl in this story.

"Turner…do you have a last name?"

His brow furrows as he fills the glass coffee pot with water from the sink. "Just Turner." Turning on his socked feet, he heads to the refrigerator on the opposite wall. "How's your head?"

Subject is obviously not a fan of eye contact. He's doing everything to avoid it.

I brush my fingertips over the knot on my head and wince. "Okay, I guess…a little sore."

Pulling out a bag of coffee grinds, he lays it on the counter. "Advil in that drawer"—he points to the drawer of the cabinets closest to me—"Ice in the freezer."

"No, thank you. Ice and I are no longer on friendly terms. So, umm, I take it you don't have a landline…"

"Nope."

"When do you think this storm will let up? You know—since my phone has no signal"—once again, I glance down at the phone in my hand. Yup, zippo—"and your television doesn't seem to be working." I motion to the room with the TV with the hockey puck stuck in the middle of it.

"Maybe a day or two," he grunts while he pours the grinds into the filter and turns on the pot.

"A day or two?!"

He makes a face, implying I'm taxing his nervous system. Or his hangover. Whatever.

"Maybe more."

"More!"

No way. No freaking way am I staying holed up in the *Amytiville Horror* house with this guy. A stranger. When nobody I know knows where I am. I've seen too many true crime documentaries to know this never ends well for the female.

He motions to the coffee pot with his chin. "Only one bathroom working so you'll have to wait till I'm done.

Help yourself to anything in the refrigerator. Cups above the sink."

Chapter Five

"Subject seems ornery," I mutter sotto voce. "Not much for verbal communication…" The way he looks at me comes to mind: apathy with a mix of annoyance. "Plenty of non-verbal, however. He glares like a champ."

I've been on the couch attempting to read for the past three hours with little to show for it. I'm still on chapter five and not because the book isn't good. It's because I'm having a hard time concentrating with Turner, the mystery gay mountain man, behind closed doors down the hall.

He disappeared into one of the other rooms three hours ago and hasn't surfaced since. In the meantime, I've located the bathroom and done my best to clean up and that's not saying much. I need my stuff and my stuff is out there somewhere…in the mother-of-all-storms.

One thing's for sure, I don't need to worry about being violated; it looks like I have the tip of an unimpressive penis growing out the side of my forehead. A mildly purplish-red protrusion. No exaggeration, it looks like a bell end. No amount of makeup is disguising it.

The door to the mysterious room opens and Turner emerges covered in fresh paint, gaze cast on the floor, his expression indicating he's in deep thought. He lumbers past the couch scratching—swear to God—something in the vicinity of his groin. Thankfully, over his sweatpants. Ignoring me, he walks into the kitchen.

"Hungry?" I hear him shout.

Am I hungry? As my Nan would say, "Does a bear shit in the woods?"

When I cross the threshold, he's washing his hands at the sink.

"Starving. I'll eat anything." Then I rethink my answer. "Except beef jerky. I don't eat beef jerky of any variety." Sliding onto one of three folding chairs at a 70s looking green vinyl kitchen table, I watch him pull out paper plates and napkins out of the cabinet above the sink. A couple of red Solo cups.

"Beef jerky?" He makes a face.

"Yeah, do you have any?"

The confused expression persists. "No."

"Good."

I checked out the refrigerator earlier. It's packed with

fresh produce. Nice to know my host is well-prepared to weather out the storm. Hopefully, he's willing to share because judging by his size he must eat an unseemly amount, and I didn't want to take anything without his express permission. Something about him tells me he's one Facebook post away from building a pipe bomb and driving to D.C. and I'm not about to do anything to anger him.

"Did you have anything for breakfast?" he asks as he peers into the open fridge, the massive width of his shoulders obscuring everything inside.

"No. I didn't want to disturb whatever you were doing—"

"Painting. And I told you to help yourself to anything you wanted."

Painting? This guy seems about as sensitive as an anvil. "Like...the walls?"

Looking over his shoulder, the glare he levels at me is a full-bodied one. This is not his usual glare-lite. This one means to intimidate. I'm guessing he found my question offensive. "No."

"Sorry..." I mutter. "I might have a concussion. Everything that's coming out of my mouth today sounds wrong."

He pulls a loaf of sliced wholegrain bread out of the refrigerator and places it on the counter, follows it up with three bags of cold cuts, tomatoes and lettuce.

"Turkey or roast beef?"

"Turkey please."

"Mayo or mustard?"

"Mustard."

Turner moves around the kitchen with the ease of someone who's comfortable preparing a meal. A few minutes later he places a plate in front of me. On it sits a perfectly made turkey sandwich sliced in two, bread lightly toasted, a bag of potato chips next to it. It looks and smells so good I can barely wait to sink my teeth into it.

"This is delicious. Thank you," I say around a mouthful. "And thanks again for saving me." He grunts in answer as he bites into his sandwich. "How did you find me, by the way?"

He puts his sandwich down and wipes his hands on the napkin. "Dumb luck. I was asleep on the couch and your headlights came through the window and hit me in the face."

Dumb luck is right. Talk of the car reminds me that I need my toothbrush and a fresh pair of underwear

ASAP. "Turner...I need my things. From the rental."

He blinks, expression blank. Then he scowls and shakes his head. "It's too dangerous for you to go out there."

Yeah, I know. I'd probably never find my way back. "I need certain things in that luggage. Important things."

"Nothing more important than your life."

I'm glad he thinks so.

"You don't understand..." I say softly, imploring him to understand with my eyes.

Sighing tiredly, he places his elbows on the table and claps his hands. "You want me to go get your stuff."

"That would be really nice of you."

He picks up the remains of his second sandwich and pops it in his mouth. Chewing, he cranes his neck to see out the window. "It's still coming down pretty hard. You can borrow something of mine."

This one was clearly not raised to be a gentleman, so I decide it's time for the nuclear option. "Flo's in town, Turner. So unless you can lend me some tampons..." I shrug. "I need my stuff."

It takes my grouchy host thirty minutes to walk sixty feet to the end of his driveway, rescue my suitcases out of the orange Cube, and return.

Slamming the front door shut, he drops my bags at my feet and glares at me. That's alright, I can barely see with the blast of freezing cold air making my eyes water. Shivering and teeth chattering, he strips off his coat and gloves, kicks off his Timberlands.

"Thank you. I really appreciate it."

All I get in return is silence. After which, he disappears again.

* * *

Two bars. That's all the service I have by early evening as the storm moves out of the area leaving behind flurries and an enormous pile of snow.

In the meantime, I managed to take a hot shower. It's official, he's gay. I found Moroccan Oil shampoo and a rainbow bath towel in the decrepit bathroom. For a mountain man, he sure has expensive taste in hair products. The towel looked familiar. It was the same one he had wrapped around his shoulders last night.

After the shower, I wrapped my hair in buns and put on clean clothes, layering Jackie's already ruined sweater on top. On closer inspection, this place hasn't improved in cleanliness, and I don't want to ruin any more clothes that don't belong to me.

By nightfall, I am so out-of-my-mind bored that I

begin to live dangerously—I knock on the door of the room Turner is hiding behind. I figure maybe a little conversation will help kill time, and he did make me arguably the best turkey sandwich I've ever tasted.

"What," the grouch calls out.

This does not bode well but I persist. "It's Carrie… Anderson. Can I come in?" Am I curious about what he's doing in there? You bet. I mean, who is this guy really? An artist? Why does he live here? Does he have a boyfriend? What's his story? And God knows I love a good story. Is he equally curious about me? Probably not.

"Suit yourself," I hear an eternity later.

Slowly, I turn the knob and peek my head in. The room is large and well lit. Stretched canvases populate the room, leaning against the walls, on the floor. They are everywhere. Some virgin, others covered with tarps. Yikes. He must be really bad at this if he's covered all the finished paintings with tarps.

I step inside and find Turner by a large window standing in front of an easel and side table. He's in the process of cleaning a brush with a rag.

"Do you need something?" he says without looking at me.

An abandoned stool sits close to the door. I stroll over

and lean my butt against it. "No, I'm just…really bored and I can't seem to concentrate enough to read."

Glancing around, I take note of all the different paint staining the old wood floor, the rolls of linen stacked against the wall. "Is this what you do for a living? You're an artist?"

"Not for a living…but I do sell them."

Which begs the question,"What type of art?" I mean, he has them all covered up. He's clearly broke; this house is the pits. He's probably not selling many….and I ate his food. I'll send him a check when I get back on my feet, I decide.

"Landscapes mostly." He's still not looking my way, and I'm getting the acute feeling that I'm bothering him.

"Did you always want to be a painter?" A memory jumps out. Of me gathering the personal items on my desk and shoving them in the worn-out LL Bean tote I've had since high school. The look on the security officer face as he watched. I may as well have been at Harry Winston planning a heist. A chasm opens up in my chest. This is really not how I saw my life going.

"No…played hockey for a while."

"Oh, yeah? I could see that."

He looks my way for the first time since I interrupted

his work. "You can see what?"

"You playing hockey." It certainly makes more sense than Turner, the sensitive artist. Although he does have the tortured thing down pat. "Your size—for one thing. Were you any good?"

All I know about hockey is that most players are large, bearded, and have missing teeth. In other words, nothing that interests me.

"I was alright." He goes back to cleaning his brushes.

"We can't all be superstars, right?"

"Right," he answers, and if my eyes don't deceive me, tightly.

A full two minutes pass without a word exchanged. Conversation is akin to waterboarding for this guy, and I'm losing the will to try.

"What do you do?" he finally says and part of me feels a tickle of pride. Getting him to engage is no small feat, and I accomplished it.

This is how low my standards have sunk. That I get a thrill out of this guy reluctantly asking me a question.

I watch him arrange tubes of color, his fingers smeared in bright blue, red, a rich royal purple. He dips a rag in a clear solution and wipes his fingers clean with it.

"I'm a reporter," I automatically answer. Because I

still am—regardless of what Ben or his overlord think of me.

Standing upright, Turner's head whips around, his speculative gaze meeting mine. "A reporter?" His face takes on a peculiar expression.

"Uh-huh, yep. A reporter." I'm not about to explain all the failings of my life to a stranger. I can barely explain them to myself.

"You're a reporter?" he repeats, expression morphing into borderline disbelief with a side of simmering anger.

This is weird.

For a second I question whether he recognizes me from my profile picture. Heck, maybe the guy is an NFL fan and was following the story. "Umm, yeah," I reply with less confidence. Lord help me if he's on Twitter. I really don't want to hear all the things he would do to the holes in my body. I'm pretty sure I wouldn't like it.

His eyes narrow as he silently stares at me. This is probably the worst glare he's leveled at me thus far and it's beginning to worry me. He finishes cleaning his paint-stained hands with the rag and slaps it down on the cart. Then he squares up, turning to face me, hands on his hips, his sweatpants dropping below his hipbones. And I can say with absolute certainty that having this man's undivided attention is not something anyone would want.

"Who sent you?" he growls, his voice raspy to the power of ten.

That's a curveball I wasn't expecting. I'm not sure what to make of this question. Or his demeanor. "What do you mean?"

He takes one step closer and my back goes stiff. Slowly, I push off the stool and stand, fight or flight kicking in. I'll go with flight.

"Who sent you? Who do you work for?"

This is starting to get seriously scary. The Uni-Bomber gag was only a gag until this very minute. "No one. No one sent me," I answer, head shaking, my heart thumping loudly under my breastbone. Without thought, I carefully throw a sideways glance over my shoulder to the wide open door and calculate how far I can get in my Pumas in multiple feet of snow should the need arise.

"Bullshit—" He takes another step forward and stops, every muscle in his body taut. This is not looking good for me. "Tell me right now who sent you or I'll throw you out."

WTF?? In the middle of a snowstorm? At night? Most chilling is the deadly quiet tone he's using. I'm vacillating between disbelief and outright pants-crapping fear. This guy is unhinged. I knew there was something wrong with him.

And yet something has happened in the last 72 hrs that has altered my genetic makeup. Because a growing sense of anger at the injustice of it all is trying to shove the fear aside. I refuse to shrink from this. I've done a lot of shrinking lately and this is where it stops. He may do his worst, but he will not see me cower.

"Look, pal, I don't know what you're talking about, so let's calm down—"

"Don't tell me to calm down," he snipes back. "I am so sick of you people. I want to know who sent you."

"I swear, no one sent me."

His eyes narrow into two indigo slits. "Tell me or I'll toss your ass out."

Huh? My jaw is hanging. This guy is certifiable. A real nut job. Another wave of anger hits me. "No one sent me, you psycho! Who would send me anyway? No one!"

He balks at my calling him a psycho. As if I'm the first person to ever do that. Yeah, right. And I've got a bridge in Brooklyn to sell you.

He regroups quickly, however, and shakes off the surprise. "You're lying."

That's when I lose it. "The FBI sent me! Okay? That's who. And if you hurt me, if you harm a single hair on my head, they'll put you in jail for life!"

I've scored another direct hit. He rocks back on his fluffy socks, and doubt flashes on his face. "The FBI?"

"That's right, they're onto you. They're probably searching your social media as we speak. I'm sure you'll be very popular with the rest of your ilk in jail."

Now he looks baffled with a side of annoyed. "What?"

"You heard me."

The glare is back as he quietly studies me. And even though there's a stillness to him that is meant to make him appear relaxed, I don't buy it one bit. The only reason why I haven't sprinted out of the room yet is because he hasn't moved from his spot in the middle of it.

"Let me see your press creds."

Press credentials…I turned those in when they fired me. And if he realizes I no longer have the protection of an important employer, he may take liberties. "No."

That forbidding face registers my answer. "Let me see 'um."

My pulse is racing like a runaway horse, but I will

not shrink. I shake my head. "No. That's none of your business."

"Let me see them or I will put you out right now."

I've had just about enough. "It is snooowwwwing, crazy man! You know, the white stuff that almost killed me. Is that what you've been planning all along? To kill me and turn me into beef jerky? Freezings my meat for later use! My family is expecting me so don't think for a minute you're going to get away with it!"

He blinks. Other than that, he doesn't move a muscle. "Jesus fucking Christ, no one is…"—he makes a face—" going to turn you into"—he snorts—"beef jerky. You said you're a reporter." His voice has fallen a few decibels, softer, less accusatory. "What's the problem with you showing me your credentials?"

He's not luring me into his trap. I'm not the dumb girl in this story. "You have no right to demand my credentials."

"Listen up…" He exhales loudly and rakes his fingers through his hair. "I saved your life, I fed you, I nearly lost a pinky to frostbite trying to get your damn tampons from the car. You're my guest and I'm asking to see your credentials. Cough 'um up."

All those things are true. Also true, there is no reason

for him to see them.

"I can't."

"Yes, you can."

"No, I can't," I say, thinking quickly. "They're in the glove compartment of the rental."

The vein running up his forehead looks ready to explode. "Are you kidding?"

"No." That's partly the truth. I'm not kidding—I'm lying.

His head drops and he takes a deep breath.

Although the snow is falling more gently and the worst of the storm has passed, the conditions outside are still far from safe. In fact, it looks like there's a solid five feet of snow banked up to the window. Wading through it to get to the car is no easier now than it was this afternoon.

"Fine. I'll get them." He starts for the door, brushing past me, and alarm bells start ringing in my head—a five alarm fire drill.

"You can't go out there!" I shout, running after him.

"Done it two times already."

He makes it to the front door and shoves his feet in the Timberlands sitting on the mat. If he gets out there and finds the glove compartment empty, he may very well tear me limb from limb. I can't risk it. I can't risk angering him any more than he already is.

The stress has me on the verge of tears as I watch him throw on his heavy Northface coat.

"Wait!" He freezes, not glancing my way at first. "You can't go out there."

Now he faces me and rolls his eyes.

"It's too dangerous," I implore, my voice high and tight with anxiety. "I can get the creds after it stops snowing. After you plow us out tomorrow. Before my father comes to get me."

A strategic drop—the mention of my dad. To let him know that I have family who will be looking for me. Always humanize the victim. That is to say, if I play this right, I won't be a victim.

He doesn't buy it though. Grabbing the handle, he's about to open the door when the stress of the last three days catches up to me.

"I don't have any creds!"

Turning away for the door, he searches my face and the dam breaks. Tears start running down my face and I can do nothing to stop them.

"What do you mean, you don't have any?"

"I mean, I don't have any…I was laid off…last

month."

That earns me a glare-lite. "And you expect me to believe that?"

"Turner, seriously, I was fired. I don't have any."

I feel like I'm being fired all over again. How humiliating, having to explain myself to this guy. Walking back to the couch, I sit and wipe my face off with the sleeve of my sister's ruined pink cashmere sweater. When the quiet gets too much to bear, I glance up again.

He watches me for one, two, three excruciating silent moments. "Why?"

"Why what?"

"Why were you fired?" His tone does not evoke warm fuzzies or the desire to pour my heart out. In fact, he sounds more annoyed and inconvenienced than ever.

"Oh…uh…" I'm too emotionally drained to come up with a plausible excuse on the fly. "A tweet. I was fired over a tweet."

Turner slips out of his coat and hangs it back up on the row of hooks on the wall. He kicks off his boots. "What did you tweet?"

"What difference does it make?"

"I'm still deciding whether to believe you," he barks.

"Now, what was it?"

It's my turn to sigh tiredly. "A story I broke years ago…on the quarterback of the Dallas Stars, Halpern. He—"

"—died a month ago. I know." Crossing his arms, he studies me. "You broke the story on him four years ago?"

For the first time since we've met, Turner looks less than pissed off and more than curious. I nod, dry my eyes again.

"And?"

"And management didn't approve of the tweet I sent out on the day of his accident." I look away, at my knuckles, red from the cold. "They got a lot of blowback…I'm sorry if that upsets you." Frustrations bubbles up again. I'm not ready to surrender to this sour, high-handed, possibly-violent jerk. "I'm sorry he beat the shit out of a woman that weighed less than his Rottweiler. And I'm sorry he's not the hero you wish he was. I only report the news—I don't make it." That has me thinking about everything that's happened since I returned to New York. "At least—I try not to."

Turner shakes his head. "I feel for his family, but he wasn't the person his fans thought he was."

The phrasing gets my attention. "You say that as if

you knew him." There's no chance a loner living in a rundown farmhouse on the outskirts of Lake Placid would ever cross paths with a hundred million dollar Super Bowl winning quarterback.

Turner walks away, heading straight for the room where he "paints." Right before the door closes, I'd swear on a Bible that I hear him say, "I did."

Chapter Six

THE TRI-LAKES REGION, MADE up of Lake Saranac, Placid, and Tupper, has a rich history. Here's some trivia for you, President Calvin Coolidge made White Pine Camp the summer White House in 1926, and the Lakes hosted two Winter Olympics. The first in '32 and the last in '80.

A bonafide sports factory, the area in general has been pumping out pro athletes for decades. Over two-dozen of them competed in the Vancouver Games and almost a dozen in Sochi. And many of them still return to train here when they're not competing.

Lake Saranac in particular became popular in the 1800s as the preferred destination of the famous and wealthy who were fighting and recovering from tuberculosis. The *Cure Cottages*, as they were called, became temporary homes for writer Robert Louis Stevenson and composer Bela Bartok, among many others.

My great great Swedish ancestors (somewhere along the way we lost an extra s) purchased one of these properties. However, once the tuberculosis vaccine was discovered, the cottages lost their appeal, and it was repurposed as a hotel.

Comfort Cottages has been in my family for four generations. And after everything that's happened in the last week, I'm reminded that I've always sort of taken it for granted that it would always be here to catch me if I fell.

Well, I've fallen.

Turner's Expedition slowly chugs up the cleared driveway of the hotel and a small buzz swirls in my gut. Being back here feels less than a punishment and more like a personal challenge. That's good, I guess.

While Turner pretends I don't exist, I examine the man who both saved my life and made it a living hell the last two days. Head cocked back, muscular arm extended, one big hand resting on top of the steering wheel. His expression says one thing only—back off.

I'm happy to, pal. I'm happy to back way off.

He woke up early and told me to get dressed. Then he handed me a shovel and the two of us—okay, mostly him—shoveled the porch. After which he pulled out the snowblower and cut a path wide enough to drive his Expedition to the main road. He didn't say one word to me other than, "Maybe hit the gym once in a while," after I got tired and had to sit to catch my breath.

I revise my prior assessment of him being a cousin to the Uni-Bomber. He's not dangerous, just mean for whatever reason. He's more Ebenezer Scrooge. Yep, Ebenezer Scrooge of the Adirondack Mountains has a nice ring to it.

A hot Scrooge—because fair is fair.

Which doesn't matter because Scrooge and I will be parting ways forever as soon as he drops me off. "How did you know?" I ask, unsure whether I'll get an answer.

Frankly, it's less a question and more an accusation. I gave him the address and he drove straight here without needing direction or GPS.

"Google map."

The sly passing glance he gives me earns him an involuntary eye-roll.

Whatever, Scrooge.

Dad's outside gathering wood for the fireplaces when we pull up to the main house, a big twenty-room, white Victorian with glossy navy-blue shutters. It serves as reception and the family residence, hosts weddings and banquets. A smile lights up his face when he sees the SUV approach.

We park out front and Turner gets out of the Expedition "Gene," he says, tipping his head at my father.

"Jake," Dad says, not missing a beat.

Gene? Jake? Wtf?

Dad's attention shifts to me. "Carebear! How's the head?"

Reaching up, I brush my fingers over the unicorn next to my temple. Yeah, it's still there. "I'll live. Hi, daddy."

Slipping out of the Expedition, I walk into my father's open arms. Out of the corner of my eye, I catch Turner watching us. Our eyes meet and he ducks his head. Opening the back door, he takes my suitcases out.

"How are you?" I ask, glancing up at my father.

"Good, now that you're home."

Turner brushes past us and deposits my stuff on the porch, and I level my so-called good Samaritan with an accusing squint. "Jake?"

And get another glare-lite for this. It's like his calling card at this point; he's never without it.

"You two know each other?" I ask my father, my attention bouncing back and forth between him and the man I'm developing unchristian-like feelings for.

"Carrie! You had us worried sick," my grandmother calls out.

She appears at the top of the stairs, looking exactly as she did the last time I saw her two years ago, when they came to visit. She's wearing her standard issue red turtleneck with a fair isle sweater over it, jeans, and her hair is the same shellacked white helmet. To complete the outfit, a skinny cigarette is tucked between two fingers in one hand and Elvis, her Main Coon, is tucked under the opposite arm. Seeing me, he hisses. Freaking hell spawn.

"Sorry, Nan."

"Hi Martha," I hear Scrooge call out.

"Hi Jake," my grandmother chirps back. "Did you take care of my baby girl?"

"Promised I would," he tells her.

I feel like the dumb girl in this story. Apparently everyone is in the loop but me. And if it's one thing that ticks me off, it's being out of the loop. "What is going on here?"

"Jake lives here, sweetie," Dad proudly announces, tucking me closer. Then his attention pivots back to Jake. "You didn't tell her?"

"Thought it be a nice surprise."

Yeah, I bet he did. The glare I give him should've cooked his flesh to medium-well. Doesn't seem to make much difference, however. Completely unbothered, he turns on his heels and heads for the cottages without another word while I watch him go.

"He lives here?" I repeat, my voice loaded with genuine disappointment.

"Moved in last summer."

I suspect there's more to this story, but I need a shower and wifi, stat.

"Can I stay in the Austen?"

All the cottages are named after Zelda's favorite authors. Why my father never changed them is beyond me. If my husband walked out on me, I'd do my best to erase him from my life.

"Yep. It's the only cottage available," Dad says, smiling down at me.

There are more creases around his eyes, more grey peppers his dark brown hair, and yet he's still as handsome as ever.

My father could easily pass for a movie star. Better looking than Cary Grant, someone wrote in his yearbook. Although Dad is definitely more Jimmy Stewart than Cary Grant. He's a simple guy, my dad. There's nothing flashy about him. He doesn't need much to be happy and never aspired to anything more. Which is weird because Zelda was never happy with anything. What draws people in is his utter sincerity, his humility, his kindness. He's completely comfortable with who he is. Probably why Zelda had to have him. She feeds on other people's kindness.

"Which one is he staying in?" I ask as I watch Turner's back disappear around the corner. "Wait, let me guess—the Poe?"

"The Hemingway."

Dammit. That's the one next to mine.

* * *

"What are your plans, now that you're back?"

The dreaded parental third-degree. I knew it was coming. Nan made dinner, her signature meatloaf, and I'm shoveling down the third slice when it starts. I look across the kitchen table with my fork suspended in mid-air. My father's expression is carefully neutral…for now.

Behind him, hanging on the wall, a new painting keeps stealing my attention. It's a winter landscape, austere and minimalistic but stunning in its simplicity. My eyes keep wanting to rest there.

"Nice painting."

"You should tell Jake. It's one of his," Dad casually informs me.

The surprise it written on my face. Wow, I'm batting a big fat goose egg with that guy. He's not a bad painter, he's an amazing one. "Eh, hard pass."

"Why exactly did ya get fired?" Nan cuts in. Her expression is far from neutral. While Dad treads softly, Nan stomps around a topic with steel toed combat boots and kicks it in the balls.

"Umm…a tweet." I fill my mouth and chew. Stalling is my friend right now.

"A tweet?" my grandmother barks back.

"Yeah, you know—Twitter. Have you heard of it, Nan?"

"Is that what the President does? Sending those little messages?"

This has all the makings of a super awkward conversation. "Uh, yeah, pretty much."

"You lost your job over one of those little messages?" she repeats in total disbelief. Nan is turning 81 in July. She thinks the "world has gone to shit," as she repeatedly tells me. I don't blame her one bit.

"Yep."

"What did you tweet?" Dad says, jumping back in,

his attention on me too acute for comfort.

"I...I...Remember when I broke the story out of college?"

"The quarterback? The one who beat his wife?" Dad adds.

"Girlfriend. Yes." Dad's not much of a football fan. Baseball and NASCAR have always been his thing. "He died in an accident two months ago and...and I posted the article I wrote. I tried to remind people that he wasn't exactly a great guy."

Silence. I don't hear a peep out of them for two whole minutes. In the meantime, I'm sweating. This could go either way. What will not happen is that we'll just move on to a different topic. Because if there's one truth I would stake my life on, it's that nobody ever keeps their opinions to themselves in my family.

"You lost your job because you told the truth?" Nan is a freaking role model. "What kinda shit is that?" Except for the cussing. Nan cusses a lot.

"Mother..."

I'm convinced Gene was an anointed saint in a past life. I've never heard him utter a single off-color word or remark.

"What? I'm sorry if it offends your lily white

sensibilities, son, but this country is officially dead if a person can lose a job for being truthful."

"When did this happen?" Dad doesn't look as convinced of my righteousness as Nan.

"The day of his accident. Everyone on social media was talking about it."

"Carrie..."

"Dad, they were talking about his Super Bowl wins instead of the fact that he beat a woman."

"The man has family, Carrie. Parents—maybe siblings. Was he married?"

As a matter of fact, he had gotten married. I remember the shock of seeing the wedding pictures on TMZ and the Daily Mail. He tied the knot six months after winning his third Super Bowl, a mere year and a half after the arrest.

I absently nod.

"I'm not defending the guy, sweetie. He hurt a woman and the law should've seen to an appropriate punishment. But think of his family...they're blameless in all this. They're the ones you hurt by going after him."

Dad and his moral high ground. I can always count on him to make me feel like a gutter rat.

"Dad, I don't want to discuss this anymore. I honestly

don't think I did anything wrong and they fired me for it."

A moment of silence falls once again. Then Dad sighs. "Well, I need help around here. Maggie's retirement snuck up on us."

"She told us last year," Nan announces, throwing Dad under the bus. Then she winks at me and I bite the inside of my cheek to hide the smile.

"Be that as it may, I didn't prepare for it. Maybe I was in denial. Maggie did everything around here…" Dad leans back in his chair and takes a sip of his craft beer. "I'll pay you half of what I was paying her."

That's almost as much as I was making at my old job. Journalism does not pay in the monetary sense. And without the expense of rent, I can build a nice little savings account pretty quickly. Which means I can move back to L.A. faster than I had anticipated. The worst is finally behind me.

"Throw in health insurance and we have a deal."

* * *

By ten, I'm back at the Austen, showered, and tucked in bed scrolling through my Twitter account. I don't know why I continue to torture myself with it, but I do. As painful to revisit as they are, I read each and every one of the life-threatening direct messages and nasty comments and start blocking those accounts. I refuse to cave to the vicious mob and delete my account. It would imply that I did something wrong and despite what my father thinks I don't believe I did. Besides, If you can't stand the court of public opinion, you have no business being in a line of work that gets you this level of scrutiny.

The sound of the shower running gets my attention. It's coming from the wall that my headboard butts up against.

Turner…Jake…Scrooge, whatever, is turning in early. Or maybe he has a gentleman friend coming over. God help that poor soul. And God help me if I have to listen to them doing the dirty.

The cottages were built in pairs, sharing a common wall, which unfortunately leaves little to the imagination. Another sound, that of the toilet flushing, makes me yearn for ear plugs. I make a mental note to include disposable ones in the welcome basked for guests.

The thought of Turner entertaining someone piques my curiosity, however. This is usually quite easy to accomplish, but until this moment I hadn't had the time nor the wifi available to pursue that lead.

With his sparkling personality, I can't imagine him

trying to pick someone up. Nope, it has to be in a way he doesn't have to speak and consequently scare the poor guy off. He's probably on Grindr. Yep, he seems like the lazy sort. Swipe and go would be his style.

Grabbing my laptop, I Google search *Jake Turner hockey player* and what comes up has my jaw dropping and a current of awareness riding up my back.

Holy Swedish meatballs…Jake Turner is famous. And not just famous, he's an actual superstar.

Hundreds of pictures populate the screen. Of Turner scoring, of him jumping over the penalty box railing, of him hoisting the Stanley Cup…and smiling. Oh my God, Turner is capable of smiling. And he has teeth. Nice teeth.

His words come back to me, "I'm alright." Alright, my ass. MVP this, biggest contract in the NHL that. That lying sack.

Another picture catches my attention. The one below it. The one of an overturned, crumpled black Jeep smashed against a copse of trees. I click on it and an article pops up. The headline reads…

MIKE BRESLER, CAPTAIN OF THE STANLEY CUP WINNING TEAM, THE BOSTON BEARS, DEAD AT 36. JAKE TURNER, LEAGUE MVP, IN STABLE

CONDITION.

Sitting up abruptly, I open every article about the accident and minimize the pages. Then I begin to read, my eyes devouring article after article, trying to glean as many actual facts as possible.

The speculations I find in most of them are nauseating and quickly tossed aside, but the facts remain that Bresler and Turner, long time friends, were driving in a remote area of Oregon, headed to Bresler's fishing camp the day after their Stanley Cup win.

The police report states that Turner was driving late at night when a deer crossed the road. The Jeep, which was traveling at 75 mph, flipped multiple times when Turner swerved to avoid it. The two weren't reported missing by Bresler's wife until the next day. By then, Bresler was found dead, thrown from the car, and Turner was clinging to life with internal injuries.

There's a lot of blame levied at Turner. A lot of talk about him being extremely drunk and possibly high when they left for the airport. Apparently they chartered a flight to Oregon that same night and picked up Bresler's Jeep at the private airport. Though nothing was proven and the police report doesn't indicate any foul play. Still, scrolling through some Twitter stories, it's clear a large swath of NHL fans believed he was responsible for Bresler's death.

My heart is racing and all I can do is stare at the white wall that separates the Austen from the Hemingway. It all makes sense now.

I scan the article for a date. The accident happened in June, the day after they hoisted the Stanley Cup, four years ago…which works out to be exactly one month before my story broke.

Chapter Seven

I was ten when my mother decided to leave us for a woman and move to New York City without explanation. Word spread fast and had two very dramatic effects.

One, my father was suddenly very popular with every divorcée and widow in town, all of them desperate to play therapist slash lover. Which inevitably made Jackie and me targets of a lot of unwanted attention. Jackie had no problem icing everyone out; nobody does bitch better than Jackie. In contrast, I fell prey to every kid's mom who invited me over for after school playtime. Even when their child hated me and told me so repeatedly.

The second effect was that kids being kids, tortured me. My father having to explain that a woman can love another woman and live as a family is something I'll never forget. It was mind boggling to me, taking me forever to reconcile. Jackie tried in her own way to explain it to me, but all I did was argue with her that it couldn't be true because I'd never seen a family with two moms. In my ten-year-old head, Zelda had my dad. What could she possibly need another woman for?

That year pretty much set the stage for the next seven. Kids started to exclude me from birthday parties and after school events. And before long I was eating lunch at school by myself.

All that changed in the eighth grade, when Gina Polizzi moved into town. Originally from Staten Island, her big Italian family had moved here to open a pizza shop. None of my classmates made any effort to get to know her. But having been raised with four brothers, Gina had no boundaries and no problem taking a seat at my table without invitation. We hit it off immediately.

We banded together over our shared mutual misery, our love for Sex and the City, and a healthy dislike of anything sports related. Two outliers whose only sin was not being pretty enough or thin enough or unique enough to fit in with the jocks, or the cool kids, or the computer nuts.

Gina had a quick tongue and a happy-go-lucky-attitude so most of the kids didn't mess with her the way they did me. I attached myself to her like a barnacle. Unfortunately for Gina, allowing me to attach myself meant she was ostracized too.

The next day, with great trepidation, Nan lends me her 1972 baby blue Mercedes and I take a trip into town. Time to rip off the Band-Aid. The more I postpone facing the people who still live here, the worse it'll feel.

My first stop, the supermarket to pick up a few essentials.

I'm pushing the cart down the cereal aisle, lazily browsing, when Jackie calls.

"What the actual fuck," she says as soon as I answer.

"No kidding." Because we both know she already got the story out of my father.

"Tell me everything."

"Everything? That would require four hours and three cocktails."

"Okay, the highlights then. What were you thinking driving through a nor'easter?"

In my line of sight, I spot a woman leaving the store and freeze, questioning my eyes. Tall, thin, chin length brown hair…

"Hello?" she adds when I don't answer fast enough.

"Sorry. I just saw a woman that looks a lot like you-know-who."

"Nah. She's in New York," my sister assures me. "She just did the View…" It sure as hell looked like her.

"Carrie? You didn't answer my question. Were you high driving in those conditions?"

That snaps me out of my musings.

"I was thinking that my credit cards are maxed out and my sister didn't let me move in with her."

"Carrie—"

"Whatever. I got my revenge. Your pink cashmere sweater is trashed, bitch."

She snorts and it makes me smile. I miss her already. "How's the baby?"

"Fine." She doesn't elaborate and I don't push. "Dad said some guy named Jake saved you? Sounds exciting. What happened?"

A storyboard of images from the past few days comes to mind, and I almost giggle. How can I possibly explain? So I strip it down to the bare bones. "Basically, I crashed the rental in his driveway out on 73, he pulled me out of the car, and I was stuck at his place for two days."

A moment of silence follows.

"I can barely get you to shut up most of the time and you choose now to be cryptic? What's he like?"

I think of the turkey sandwich Turner made me. "He's got a mean streak a mile wide."

"Yikes. That doesn't sound like any fun. Is he hot?"

"Jackie..."

"What? I'm a hormonal mess. Can a girl indulge in a fantasy or two?

"Jesus Christ Superstar, you have a husband. What do you need a fantasy for?"

"Oh, baby sister, thou art so naive. I need new material for my spank bank and poor Charlie's worn out from satisfying my needs. I think I broke his dick the other day."

I nearly throw up in my mouth. "TMI. TMI times ten."

"So?"

Sighing, I stop pushing the cart and picture Turner sleeping in the recliner, the corded forearms, the groves next to his hips. No debating whether he's hot. I mean, fair is fair.

"He's hot if you like the Neaderthalish type. He's a goon. I'm convinced he's only half human. I would never be interested in him—even if he was straight. Oh, and he's gay, by the way. So if that's your kink, you can haaa..." My voice fades as I turn to grab a box of Cheerios I passed along the way.

And nearly run right into Turner, a basket full of fresh fruits and vegetables hanging from his hand, an expression of pure contempt on his face. Dressed in black running pants and a black thermal for maximum intimidating effect no doubt.

"Jackie, I gotta go." I hang up on my sister without waiting for a response, my voice cracking as a lump of regret fills my throat. There's no speculating whether he heard me—the look on his face says it all.

All the blood in my body rushes to my face. "Turner…"

He breaks eye contact for a moment, long enough to glance around to see if we're alone. "I'm not gay—not that it's any of your business."

"Turner…" I want to apologize, but the words won't come out. They stop halfway up my throat. I'm so embarrassed I lose the power of speech.

He steps closer and his chin comes down. Close enough that I can smell soap and Moroccan Oil shampoo from a recent shower. Close enough that I have to tip my head back to look at him, and as much as I want to hide, as much as I want the floor beneath my feet to crack open and swallow me whole, I force myself to look up at him.

"I haven't been with a woman in three years," he quietly confesses, the rasp like sandpaper on the flushed skin of my cheeks. And although his face is eerily blank, the energy coming from him is unmistakable—he hates me. And he has every right to hate me. I am so ashamed I am absolutely certain I will never wash the guilt off. "…and even on your best day, you don't tempt me"—his sapphire eyes rake up and down my body—"not even a little."

Then he walks past me while I stay rooted to the linoleum floor. Just me, my everlasting shame, and a box of Honey Nut Cheerios.

* * *

If elementary school was hard for me, high school was exponentially worse. Memories of it are likely to trigger a panic attack so I seldom do it and never voluntarily.

The five year age gap between Jackie and me was huge when we were growing up. And even though she and I were never in high school together, I was constantly reminded that my drop dead gorgeous sister was at the top of the food chain, while I was more of a bottom feeder.

Having a sister that was both popular and class valedictorian meant it was a sure bet I would never measure up. Had that been the end of it, I would've probably survived high school largely unscathed.

Unfortunately, that wasn't all that was wrong with me.

I was a skinny hot mess. A late bloomer. One of those people that had to have braces way past the acceptable age. Mine came off the end of my sophomore year. Even worse, I was cursed with a bad case of cystic acne. What little self-esteem I did have, the acne pounded it into dust.

People who say you shouldn't place importance on appearance are either willfully insensitive, or have never been the object of ridicule. It is like dying by a thousand cuts. Each and every day it killed a little more of anything good growing inside of me until I hated myself. Until I couldn't stand to look in a mirror without wanting to break it. Self-loathing is an affliction that leads down a dangerous road.

Teenagers can be brutally honest and unknowingly cruel. By the time I graduated high school, the people in my grade probably couldn't tell you my first name. But if you asked them who Pizza Face was they could point to me immediately. Consequently, I spent all my free time daydreaming about getting out of this god forsaken town and reinventing myself.

Everything changed my freshman year at Arizona State. My roommate took one look at my face and said, "I can help you fix that."

That's all it took for my entire world to change. Turns out, she'd had a bout of acne too, and her mother had spent thousands on some fancy holistic doctor.

I stopped eating all processed food, dairy, tomatoes, and whole bunch of other foods that cause inflammation. It was really hard, and it didn't happen quickly, but by the end of the year my skin was completely clear with only an occasional light breakout. By then, however, the damage had already been done.

Point is, I, better than anyone, know what dunking on someone does to their psyche, their self-worth. Whether he heard me or not, I shouldn't have been talking badly about him to anyone. Was he equally mean to me? Yes. And that still doesn't excuse my behavior.

It's a testament to how many times I've been told I was unattractive, or made to feel that way, that his insult failed to leave a mark. Besides, it's not like I would ever expect someone like Turner to be attracted to someone like me. I'm cute now. At least, I think so. But despite his terrible personality, straight Turner is way, way out of my league. And I'm perfectly okay with that.

So after two sleepless nights and a lot of soul searching, I'm determined to grow some hair on my chest and apologize. To that end, I set my alarm for the ungodly hour of 4:30 a.m. That's generally the time Turner returns from his morning run around the lake, and I plan to ambush him with kindness.

On cue, a tall dark figure approaches on the path. He's wearing a black wool cap and some sort of technical running pants and jacket. A sporty Grim Reaper, if you will. Against the backdrop of a pink stained dawn, he seems even more hostile. And sexy if I'm being completely honest. My heart skips a beat.

"Showtime."

He slows to a walk and starts measuring his heart rate. That's my cue to jump out of the back of the Austen holding a bag of fresh muffins Nan made the night before.

"Hi Turner!"

Startled by my sudden appearance, his face whips around. Seeing me, he frowns. Not an encouraging start, but I persevere.

"Hi. Hi, so…I got these for you." I hold up the paper bag, which he stares at with indifference. Sadly, he looks disinclined to take it. This is not at all awkward.

"Can we talk?" He responds to this with another blank stare. "Please, it'll only take a minute."

Exhaling tiredly, he pulls the pods out of his ears… and waits.

"Yeah, so…uh, I just wanted to apologize for the other day. I shouldn't have said that. I really…I shouldn't have said it. I didn't mean it. I mean, I really *did* think you were gay. But that was obviously a mistake on my part. Not that you gave off any gay vibes or anything. Not that there's anything wrong with being gay. I love gay people—" Yikes, this is not going well. "That's all on me. I have no excuse. And I'm sorry if I hurt your feelings. Here"—I thrust the muffins at him and he unwillingly takes them—"Nan made them. Anyway, I apologize from the bottom of my heart."

Still no change in expression. Man, this guy is tough.

I wait. I wait some more. For him to accept. For him to say anything at this point. For him to show some freaking mercy. I'm freezing my butt off out here.

Wrapping my arms around myself, I jog in place, and his critical gaze rakes up and down my thermal onesey PJs, the one with smily faces on it.

"That it?" he finally bestows upon me.

This is not how I saw this going in my head. "Umm, yeah, I guess."

Then he hands me back the bag of muffins and walks

inside.

* * *

"The heck is he doing…" I murmur to myself. Because that's what I usually do when I'm spying, surveilling, whatever. Turner's out back, going back and forth from the woodshed, for the last twenty minutes.

Leaning closer to the window over the kitchen country sink, I crane my neck to watch him come out swinging an ax. For a man who despises me, he looks way too comfortable swinging an ax.

We haven't so much as shared a passing glance since the day of my botched apology a week ago. He does his best to ignore me and I return the favor.

I hear him, though. I hear him loud and clear. I hear him get up at 4 a.m. I hear the door bang shut when he goes for his daily run. I hear the shower running, and I hear the Expedition peal out of the driveway when he leaves for the farmhouse. But he's a paying guest, so I keep my mouth shut and pull the pillow over my head.

I thought about apologizing again, but that's out of the question. Every time he's anywhere near me, his electric fencing goes on and I don't want to get zapped again. I'm done with his attitude. I apologized repeatedly. If he doesn't want to accept it, too bad so sad.

Dangelico

Absently, I turn on the sink and the water sputters. Great. Something else to fix. After weeks of dealing with clogged toilets, thermostat issues, and a young couple staying in the Miller cottage keeping the neighbors up with their sexscapades, I've decided that this cannot go on much longer. My intellect will not allow it.

Which is why I've made a plan to check if the town newspaper, The Gazette, is hiring—as soon as possible.

A chill runs through me and I'm reminded to add wood to the fireplaces. This house was originally built in the 1800s and even with all the renovations Nan and Dad made over the years, it's still drafty.

Grabbing my sister's down coat and the leather carrier, I throw it on and walk out back to fetch some wood. Turner is still there—except now he's shirtless. Give me a break. Even with the sun out, it's in the 30s, which for April is completely normal. In contrast, I have so many layers on I look like the Michelin tire man.

He places a piece of wood on the stump, raises his arms above his head, muscles tensing and rippling, and comes down hard on it. Tossing the two pieces aside, he sets up another one.

"Put it away, Turner. No one here is interested." Walking past him, I reach a neat pile siting against the side of the woodshed.

"You've been staring at me from the kitchen window for the past half hour"—he brings the ax down hard, grunting as it impacts the wood—"so I beg to differ."

Heat blankets my face while I clutch my jacket like an uptight heroine from an 18th century novel. "It's more gross fascination. Like being at the zoo. Or a freak show."

I don't know what it is about this man that brings out the worst in me. Or is it the best? Whatever it is, my practically nonexistent ability to defend myself rises like a phoenix from the ashes whenever he speaks.

Turner stops and leans on the handle of the ax, chest heaving as he takes deep breaths. I look away, out yonder, but as a suspicious length of silence grows curiosity gets the best of me and I'm forced to look at him again.

A slow sinister smile transforms the brute force of his face into something not at all unappealing. And this is where things take a turn for the worse because a creeping sensation of dread fills my chest. God help me, I can't be attracted to him.

"Difference is…you can't touch those animals."

He's got me so on edge I start to walk away. Then, realizing I came out here for a reason, I make a quick U-turn. Aaand come up short when I find him standing right behind me, holding two pieces of wood.

My gaze moves up his chest, covered in a light dusting of dark hair, nipples pointing from the bite in the air. It slowly move over his Adam's apple and his tense jaw. By the time I reach his face, his expression is back to being as serious and intense as always.

Watching me intently, he places the wood in the leather carrier.

"Thank you," I force myself to mutter, because it always pays to be kind.

The quiet chuckle I hear come out of him as I walk back inside sets my teeth on edge though.

After lighting the fireplace in Dad's office, I get busy looking through the bookings for this calendar year. If you like winter sports, this is the place to be. Skiing, skating, ice hockey, hiking—we've got it all. And if sports aren't for you, there's always sightseeing and shopping. I can't recall a single winter that we haven't been packed, attracting guests from Boston, New York, even as far as Japan, and this year is no different. We're sold out until the end of March.

Carrying two coffee cups, Dad walks in having returned from his trip to the hardware store. "Everything look good?" he asks, placing one on the desk.

He knows the answer to that; Maggie always ran a tight ship.

"We're completely sold out for the winter." I don't know why I hadn't thought of it before. The Austen should've been rented out.

Nodding, he sits in his favorite wing chair by the fireplace. It brings back memories—most of them not very pleasant.

I can still see his face when he sat me and Jackie down to tell us Zelda was not coming back. I can still remember my disbelief. How I accused him of being a liar. That it was his fault she'd left. How I defended her. Shame makes me hot under the collar.

"We are."

"I don't want you to lose the income from the Austen. I can move in here."

Between the cat and Nan smoking I can't say I'm thrilled, but the alternative seems wasteful. There are three empty bedrooms upstairs.

Taking a sip, Dad watches me over the rim of his cup. "We're not losing anything. Jake rents it because he doesn't want anyone next door. He said you could have it."

My insides melt. This is terrible news. The absolute worst news possible. "He did…" I say completely forlorn. "Why is he living here, anyway? I mean, other than that farmhouse needs to be condemned."

"Don't know…" Dad shrugs. "He had plans to demo the farmhouse and build last fall and never got around to it."

It tells you the state of things between us that a random act of kindness from him evokes dread. I'm going to have to do some serious groveling. Lovely.

Chapter Eight

I saw a documentary once on Nat Geo Wild about salmons. It explained how they hatch in fresh water rivers, but spend most of their lives out to sea. Once they reach maturity, around three or four years of age, they return to the very same river guided by the magnetic field of the earth, swim all the way back upstream, reproduce, and die.

Sad as all get out. That's not my point, however.

What struck me as interesting is how pretty the salmon were when swimming downstream and living in the vastness of the great Pacific Ocean.

Their bodies evenly formed. Sleek, silver torpedos.

And in comparison, how ugly and deformed they became once they had battled innumerable elements—bears hunting for their favorite food, waterfalls, downed trees, beaver dams, shallow rivers beds—to meet their fate and keep the species alive. Their bravery and incredible feats of strength made them victors in the mating game. Their scars and misshapen heads meant that they had succeeded, and in turn, rewarded.

If only that were true of us humans.

Like a salmon swimming upstream, hardship has changed the shape of me. My insides and my outsides. At least, I claim it has.

For years, I've taken pride in the fact that I didn't let my past dictate my future. That I didn't stay mired in self-doubt and didn't make excuses for my lack of confidence. Instead, I worked hard to change it. Because I am not my history. My history is only a small part of me.

Then again, my resolve has never really been tested before. Ben and everyone else I worked with didn't know the Pizza Face kid whose mother left them for another woman. It was easy to convince them I was like everybody else when I didn't have to change their mind of who I had been.

To that end, I can't hide at the hotel forever.

The sidewalks of Main Street are crowded with locals and tourists. It's a weekday so it's not as bad as weekends and holidays, but busy nonetheless.

On the way to the offices of The Gazette, I decide to live dangerously and pop into a gourmet coffee shop and grab a latte. Running into someone, anyone, that knew me then and having to explain why I'm back is not something I want to do right now but I can't live in fear either.

As I'm walking out, stepping onto the ice and snow slicked concrete, I almost crash, latte first, into someone entering.

"Whoops, sorry," I automatically call out.

At first I don't recognize her. The sexy razor sharp pink bob. The tiny diamond stud in her nose. The perfectly applied makeup. It's all new. However, the smile and the laughter in her eyes is unmistakable.

"Gina?" I say, both surprised and happy to see her.

"Carrie? Oh my God, when did you get back?"

Throwing her arms around me, she hugs me tightly while I hold up the take-out cup to avoid spilling it all over her. The girl has not changed one bit.

"A few weeks ago."

"It's so good to see you. And I go by Regina these day. You know, since Imma business owner and a pillar of the community."

I can't stop grinning. It's not just good to see her; it's great. "Good for you. Which business?"

"Across the street," she tells me, motioning to a stately, turn-of-the-century red brick building. "The bar."

A brass sign hangs over the heavy wood and glass

door. **Queen**, it reads.

"Wow. Nice place."

"It's a lot of work, but it's mine."

"You did good," I say, taking it all in. I guess I wasn't the only one with big aspirations.

Smiling, she tugs on my sleeve. "What about you?" Despite the smile, something in her expression tells me she knows.

"You know, don't you?"

"I'm sorry," she says, cringing. "Enzo's on Twitter a lot—probably too much. He told me."

Gina's older brother. "He's a fan, I take it?"

He pert little nose scrunches and she nods. "Dallas all the way. You look great, by the way. All glowed up."

"Speak for yourself."

She's lost some of the extra weight, but her curves are still there and her face is as pretty as ever. Especially her poreless skin; it's the first thing I noticed about her when we met over a decade ago.

"I should get going. I have to open and let my crew in. Come by the bar sometime soon. I'll make you a cocktail, and we can catch up."

We part ways after I promise to come by and she hugs me again.

By the time I reach the offices of The Gazette my fingers are ice cold and my cheeks raw from the windchill. It's April and still colder than Zelda's heart.

I take my red knit hat off and make an attempt to fix my staticky hair. It's down today. Jackie would approve. Then I push on the glass door and enter reception.

A young man, early twenties, slight in build and features, glances up from his computer screen. He has light brown hair and dark brown eyes. He checks me out and offers a genuine smile. "Can I help you?"

Time to dance.

At this point I can only hope they're clueless about my scandalous behavior on Twitter. "Hi, I'm Carrie Anderson," I say, stepping forward, I place the manila envelope on the counter. "I was hoping to speak to someone about possibly working here?"

His blank, deer-caught-in-the-headlights stare leads me to rush into my pitch. "I have a BA in Journalism from Arizona State. I—"

"We're not hiring," he interrupts with an apologetic smile. "But let me get Hal, our EIC. He might know of something."

The little hope I churned up on my walk over here dwindles until I'm silently brooding. I can't even get a job at the crappy local paper.

In the meantime, the young man picks up my resume and walks to the back of the two-room office, disappearing through an open doorway. A few minutes later he waves me in. He's slim and tall, taller than Jake.

Sitting behind an ancient metal desk is a black man, thin, bald, in his late sixties is my guess, wearing wire-rimmed glasses, and a short neat silver beard. He smiles warmly and I immediately get a good feeling about him.

"Have a seat please, Miss or is it Mrs. Anderson?"

I take him up on his invitation to sit and push my coat off. "Miss. But please call me Carrie."

"I'm Hal Rodgers. Gray says you're looking for a job?"

I glance over my shoulder at Gray, and he smiles encouragingly. Maybe there's hope for me yet.

"Yes, sir." I nod, brushing my sweaty hands down the leg of my wool pants. "I graduated top of my class from Arizona State. I was EIC of The State Press, our school paper…" My voice fades away when I realize Hal Rodgers is deep in thought, staring at my resume.

Finally glancing up, he takes a deep breath and drops the paper on the desk. "I won't mince words. I'm not hiring. We're not in a good financial position. I'm bleeding subscribers. Social media has killed my readership and no one wants to see what's behind the paywall."

Down go my hopes and dreams.

"But…" he starts again. "But I'm willing to give you a shot." Resurrected, my hopes and dreams soar. "On a freelance basis. If I like what you bring me, I'll pay you for it."

Not exactly what I was looking for, but under the circumstances, I'll take the chance to prove myself.

"Hard news?" I ask even though he knows by my resume that it's clearly my lane and I should stay there.

"No," he answers, sitting forward. Elbows on the desktop, he takes his eyeglasses off and rubs his eyes. "Hard news for us is dead. Twitter killed it. We can't keep up that kind of pace." A heavy pause follows in which he examines me closely. "I want you to do a lifestyle piece. My only request is that the focus be local."

A lifestyle piece…huh. I did take that one creative writing class. "Deal," I say, rising from the chair.

"Where are you going?" Hal says, amused by my abrupt departure. Hal should smile more. The one-sided grin he's leveling at me make him look ten years younger.

"To get started. When do you need it by?"

"How does two weeks sound?"

I can't stop the grin pulling my cheeks apart. "You'll have it in one."

* * *

"You're gross. You know that, right?"

I'm talking to a cat. This is the state of my life these days. I went from cruising the Sunset strip for kicks and stories to this.

The devil's spawn is sprawled out like Caligula in front of the fireplace in my father's office licking his privates. What's particularly creepy is that he makes eye contact with me when he does it.

Almost a week has passed since my meeting with Hal Rodgers and I still don't have a topic for my lifestyle piece and it's giving me anxiety. Meanwhile, I have my other job to contend with. We're booked for a wedding in two weeks. I give that some consideration as a topic for the article. It might work. People love romance. But it doesn't excite me.

My attention pivots back to the delivery schedule. I double check when the flowers are arriving, the extra linens and chairs. Any out-of-the-norm instructions from the wedding planner. And trust me when I tell you

Carried Away

checking is important.

Once, Dad got a delivery of fifty mini butt plugs as weddings favors. Yeah, true story. We were all relieved to learn it was a mistake. It should've been mini bottle openers. Good thing we checked with the wedding planner who blamed a recently fired assistant.

Out of the corner of my eye, I can see Elvis is at it again. The fire is running on fumes so I decide to spare myself more kitty fellatio and go fetch more wood from the shed out back. Thanks to Turner, we have enough to last into my next life.

Except I'm not paying attention. I'm mulling over my article, the one that's going to blow Hal away. It's imperative I make a good impression because I may lose my mind if I'm forced to work here exclusively.

I'm stepping out of the back kitchen door when Elvis, that sneaky SOB, sensing my guard is down, makes a break for it. Horrified, I watch him trot down the back steps of the patio and gallop across the snow-covered yard.

Elvis is not an outdoor cat.

Then things to go from bad to worse as I watch him climb up the ancient birch tree next to my cottage.

"Elvis, come down. Sweet kitty..." I mutter,

swallowing the urge to verbally eviscerate him. Shivering, I wrap my arms around myself. All I have on is a wool sweater and if you ask me 30 degree weather requires a goose down comforter.

For the past ten minutes, no amount of bribery has convinced him to come down. He continues to lounge on a thick branch with his blue-gray tail lazily swinging back and forth as if he has no fornications left to give while I stare up at him with murder in my eyes.

He's taunting me. He's definitely taunting me.

"Here kitty kitty. Here you evil piece of shit. I've got tuna for you back in the kitchen."

I've been told a million times not to let the cat out, but I'm also no match for his speed and agility. Have you ever tried to herd a cat? Thus the expression *like herding cats*.

Even more troubling, I'm not sure if he's stuck up there or he's choosing to ignore me. He doesn't look scared. Just the opposite, in fact. He's sprawled out on that branch like he's king of the damn jungle.

I'm two minutes from grabbing a ladder because my grandmother cannot find out. She's in town, at the senior center for her weekly card game, and isn't expected back for another hour. She will freak if something happens to this cat. When Maeve, the female, died two years ago, I saw my Nan cry for the very first time in my entire life. She took to her bed for two days and wouldn't eat.

Nothing can happen to this cat—ever.

"Elvis please. I'm begging you." Turning his nose up, he looks disinclined to grant me any mercy. "Seriously, if you don't come down from there right this minute I'm going to go get a ladder! Get the hell down right this minute you!"

"Something tells me that's not gonna work." Turner walks up to stand next to me with two large paintings hanging from his hands. Landscapes. The first is the Adirondack Mountains in fall. The second is another winter scene. Both equally stunning.

He's dressed in black track pants and a thermal again. And unfortunately my body chooses this special moment to remind me that Turner, the Scrooge, is an incredibly sexy man…wonderful.

He catches me staring, and I look away, back up at the cat, heat inexplicably crawling up my neck. Turner's attention follows. Elvis, of course, is in the midst of licking his balls again.

"He does it all the time. It's gross," I glumly inform him. "Especially since he looks at me when he does it.

Turner makes a noise, and I turn to examine his profile. His expression is as serious as always, but I detect a subtle note of humor there, his lips pressed together to stifle a smile.

Well, well. What have we here...

"How did he get out?"

"I don't know," is my automatic reply. Which earns me a side-eye. "Okay, I may know something about it. Look, can we call a time-out on the Cold War? Tomorrow you can go back to hating my guts and stomping around as if I murdered your firstborn, but I need help right now. My grandmother will have a heart attack if she sees him up there."

His dark blue eyes catch mine, searching for something. "I don't hate your guts."

Dare I say he looks puzzled. And he actually sounds genuine. That's a two for two in the credibility department. For a moment, it knocks me off center, makes me doubt myself. What am I missing here?

"Agree to disagree," I throw out, trying to get back on track. Because I have a cat to rescue. I can't be standing here trying to solve the mysteries of what is going on in this guy's head. "So...will you help me?"

He gives me a brief nod and walks over to the porch

of the Hemingway, places the paintings against the door under the overhang. When he returns, he walks around the tree getting a measure of it.

He can't be serious.

"Don't be ridiculous, Turner. You can't climb that thing. It's too cold and slippery. And the ground is hard when you fall." The ground is covered in snow and not the fresh kind. It's days old with a thin layer of ice on it.

Turner takes a moment out of his busy schedule to scowl at me, then goes back to inspecting the tree.

"I don't want to end up in the hospital when you hurt yourself," I warn.

"Do you want my help or what?" Mr. Charm volleys back, giving me a look.

"Yes," I mutter, biting back another comment.

Against my wise counsel, Turner takes a running jump up the trunk, grabs the lowest branch, and walks up the trunk. Once he gets horizontal, he vaults up on the branch and straddles it. All this while Elvis and I watch in rapt fascination. Dressed in black workout gear and sneakers, he looks like a hot ninja. And I'm suddenly feeling a lot warmer than I was ten minutes ago.

"You were saying?" he yells down, gloating.

"I was saying that that branch is not strong enough to

hold your weight!" My heart is beating a mile a minute the way it does when danger is imminent but I can't pinpoint where it is. Call it female intuition. Or that I have a pair of functioning eyes and a brain.

"You weigh too much—like two fifty or something," I holler. "And that branch is thin! Get down. I can call the fire department. The freaking cat is a champion whatnot, a blue ribbon winner. They might come out for a celebrity."

Ignoring me, Jake scoots further down the branch and reaches out for Elvis who glances down at his rescuer with the smug satisfaction of a Marvel super villain about to unleash mayhem.

"Turner get down!"

Jake starts making kissing sounds, and if I wasn't so worried about him breaking his neck, I would say it's darn cute.

Elvis gets up from his prone position and stretches, tail wiping arrogantly back and forth. Then he takes another look at Jake and turns tail. The devil's hand puppet jumps down on a branch on the other side of the tree, leaps off the trunk, and executes a perfect landing.

I scoop him up quickly earns me a low growl. "I could kill you," I push between gritted teeth.

Once the cat is secured, my attention pivots back to the stubborn man in the tree. "Do not move. I'll be right back."

I dump Elvis in the Austen and hurry back to find Jake looking unsure how to get himself out of this mess. "I'm getting the ladder!"

"Hang on. I think I got this," he tells me, glancing left and right, his brow furrowed in deep thought.

"You do not got this!"

Does he listen? No. He swings down, hanging by his arms, then his hands, then fingers. But he's still too far off the ground to be safe.

His shirt rides up to reveal a flexed six pack, and I'm stunned into silence. That six pack has the same effect on me that a phone has on an infant. I'm in a spell. I want to explore and inspect for days on end. I want to—

"I think I need a ladder," I hear him mutter.

Now is not the time, however.

"Are you freaking kidding me! Now? Now that you're hanging by your fingertips?!"

Too late. He lets go and falls to the hard ground with a grunt. Horrified, I run over and dive to my knees. "Turner!" His face twists in pain. "Turner! Jake are you okay? I'm calling an ambulance."

I move to stand and he catches my wrist.

"Don't. I'm fine." Using me for leverage, he sits up and stretched his legs out, flexes his ankle, makes another face.

"Is it broken?! Please tell me it's not broken?"

He chuckles drily. "Help me up."

When I stand, his gaze meets mine, and for the first time, there's no cold apathy or irritation there. There's none of that. And what's even better is that there's more than a little amusement.

Holding out his hand to me, I take it and pull against his considerable weight. I throw everything I've got into it, which isn't much to be honest.

Once he's on his feet, he tests out the ankle.

"How bad does it hurt?" I can tell from the tightness around his mouth that it hurts.

"Not at all."

"Really bad, then."

"Two hundred and twenty."

"What?"

"I weigh two twenty. Not two fifty."

I find myself inspecting his body parts again. Measuring. Weighing. Yes, I know, we're not doing that anymore, we shouldn't objectify men or women. That's absolutely true. Problem is, my lonely body parts haven't gotten the memo.

He clears his throat and it jolts me out of my wayward thoughts, my gaze lifting to get a better read on him. Anyone else would believe the expression of indifference. Not me. Na. Not even a little. I can see the unspoken challenge in his eyes from a mile away.

"Congratulates. That's still too much for that branch. You could've broken your neck."

"Are you done?"

"Yes."

"Help me get to the porch?"

"Yes."

"It's only a little sore," I hear him mumble as I get closer.

He throws his arm around my shoulders, and I hold my breath. It's all I can do to contain the sigh. His weight against me, his heat, the way he smells. There's something familiar about him that I can't explain.

Once we get inside his cottage I see more paintings stacked against the wall. All finished. He releases me and hops to the refrigerator in the kitchenette, pulls an ice pack out of the freezer, and grabs a bottle of NSAIDs out of a cabinet.

"Maybe I can drive you to an Urgent Care," I say, feeling completely awkward in his personal space.

Turning, he leans his butt against the counter and slams two pills in his mouth. "I played an entire season with a fractured collar bone."

The sympathy pain I'm feeling makes me nauseous. "Oh—"

"This is nothing."

Holding onto the walls for support, he hobbles into the main room and sits on the distressed leather couch facing the bed. Which, naturally, my attention gravitates to without permission.

I can't stop picturing Turner naked, the swell of muscle, the size of him. All that tan skin beneath the white linens with the CC monogram. God help me, I'm starting to sweat. I hook a finger in my turtleneck and tug, giving myself some room to breathe.

Meanwhile, the man I'm having inappropriate thoughts about is busy kicking off his sneakers and peeling off his sock. A scar runs up the inside on the sore ankle.

"How did you do that?" I blurt out.

Putting the leg up, he places the ice pack over it and meets my eyes. He's doing it again—looking at me as if he's about to confess the secrets of the world to me and only me. Like I'm the only one he allows in his world. Which couldn't be farther from reality. Still, it's unnerving.

"Broken ankle. An old training injury."

I nod and lean a shoulder against the door jam that separates the main room from the kitchenette. Then I wait, knowing that if he wants to say more he will.

"My rookie year playing with the Bears…I didn't know if it would heal well enough for me to play again."

From the articles I read on line, I know he came from very humble beginnings. So I'm certain that not knowing whether he would remain broke, or become a millionaire was a harrowing experience.

"You got lucky, I take it?" I say in an attempt to lighten the heavy mood we're slipping under.

"Yeah."

I've never been good at letting things fester. I don't like strife of any sort. Even with Zelda. She's a constant thorn in my side because she makes me second guess whether I'm being crazy not giving her a chance.

Typically, I charge in guns blazing, or more precisely, lips flapping determined to smooth things over because I'm not okay with not being okay. Tension makes me queasy and uncomfortable.

"I'm sorry if we got off on the wrong foot…" Then I catch it, smiling. "No pun intended."

He brushes it off with a gruff, "It's fine."

"Jake…I should—I want to thank you for letting me stay in the Austen. I know you rented it to have some privacy."

"You don't have to thank me." He looks away and it dawns upon me that I may have embarrassed him.

An awkward silence falls, and I debate whether to leave. He doesn't seem as put out that I'm in his space as he was at the farmhouse. "Is your ankle any better?"

"It will be." He extends the leg and stretches it out. My eyes follow the movement and land on the bed. And I'm reminded that I'm in the room where he sleeps and… and other stuff.

"Well, I should be going…" I mutter, suddenly nervous and warm like the thermostat just got cranked up a thousand degrees. "I'll, uh, see myself out." I back away from him one step at a time while he watches. The humor under the stony façade is back. I'm pretty sure I see him fighting it. "Holler if you need anything. I mean, because of the ankle."

Goodness, I'm flubbing this.

Opening the door, I step out on the porch. He has yet to break eye contact. "Bye. And thanks again for your help with the hell raiser—Elvis, I mean. And the cottage....and, uh, for saving my life obviously." I need to shut up. "Anyway, thank you."

I shut the door behind me and take a deep breath.

Chapter Nine

ASK ANY SERIOUS SPORTS ENTHUSIAST and they'll tell you The Herb Brooks Arena, built for the 1980 Winter Olympics, is an American landmark, site of the legendary Miracle On Ice. A game that saw the heavily favored Soviet Men's Ice Hockey Team lose to a bunch of rag tag Americans 3 to 4.

When I was growing up, however, it was just the parking lot where all the high school kids would meet up to determine whose parents' booze they could steal or which house they were going to party at.

I'm following up on a lead today. One Gray mentioned in passing. Breaking news here: Twice a week the Brooks Arena is closed to the public, rented out by none other than Jake McScroogePants.

It's been a few days since the cat in the tree incident and other than him passing me by as he left for the farmhouse and my yelling in a weirdly high pitched, "Good morning," we haven't spoken.

One thing that has changed? My interest. It is

seriously piqued now, and Carrie Anderson, investigative reporter at large, did more internet digging.

The grouchy one is some kind of hockey phenom. A modern day Bobby Orr—that's what the analysts called him. Orr considered one of the all-time best. Which says a lot about the comparison.

Like Orr, Turner was a defenseman both fast and with scoring ability. Drafted at eighteen, he went second overall to the Boston Bears where he played his entire career until four years ago. I also learned that Jake never officially retired. He asked the Bears to release him from his contract.

What's even more interesting is that Turner uses the Brooks Arena to hold hockey practice for disadvantaged kids. Considering his personality, this blew my mind.

Turner and kids? Turner talking to kids? I can't imagine how.

I asked Gray to contact him for an interview and permission to let someone from the paper observe the practice session. Reluctantly, he agreed. I'm not entirely sure he would have had he known I was the one covering it. Even with our newfound truce in place we aren't exactly braiding each others hair.

Regardless, I cannot pass up the opportunity. This

article practically writes itself. Fallen Hockey God Finds Redemption Helping Kids? I literally cannot come up with a better human interest piece if I tried.

It's perfect for my article, and if I get a couple of cool candid shots I can post them on The Gazette Instagram account and Facebook page. Heck, maybe even Twitter to drive some traffic.

Inside the arena, the chill in the air makes me turtle my neck into my coat. Down below, the rink is swarming with small bodies outfitted in hockey gear. They seem to be skating in a haphazard pattern. Some taking shots on goal, some defending. I know close to nothing about the rules of hockey so I brushed up for this visit. That's not saying much, though.

In the middle of all this organized chaos, Turner stands tall on his skates, a whistle hanging from his neck, expression wolfish as he surveys his flock. On bare feet he's formidable, on skates he looks downright scary.

Good news, his ankle seems to be fine.

I walk down the stairs and sit behind the penalty box. Spotting me, he does a subtle double-take, confirming that Gray didn't tell him who was covering the story when he booked the appointment.

He skates over to the railing in one fluid motion.

"You're with the Gazette?" I nod and give him a tight, apologetic smile. "So you're doing the story…"

It's not really a question. Although judging from the way he's examining me, he doesn't seem upset by it.

"I won't get in your way…and any questions I have I can ask when you're done."

"I don't mind questions as long as the story stays local."

Turner nods and skates away, back to the group of boys of various heights and sizes, all of whom are watching me curiously.

Blowing his whistle, he directs the boys to split up into groups and begin a series of drills. It's immediately apparent that not all of them are at the same level of play. One in particular, a rather heavier one, is having trouble with a sprint drill.

I watch, transfixed, as Turner skates up to him and tips his head down, murmuring something to the seemingly frustrated boy while the others smack talk. Pulling out my phone, I snap away.

A few close ups of man and boy in deep conversation. Some of the other kids laughing. Turner eventually reprimands the group carrying on, and pats the heavy boy on the shoulder.

Holy crap. I did not see this coming at all. I'm shocked. Absolutely flabbergasted at how easily Jake Turner, aptly named Scrooge by yours truly, communicates with these kids. And it's obvious they worship him in return. One look at their faces and you can tell they are hanging on his every word.

The drills start again. Turner skates around to each group, issuing corrections and praising what they're doing correctly. The heavy boy is playing one-on-one defense, and when his opponent makes a break for the goal, he body checks him to the hard cold ground.

Peals of little boy laughter ring out through the arena. Jake skates over to the boy on the ground and helps him to his feet. He looks to be unharmed. Other than maybe a bruise to his pride.

But most of my attention is elsewhere, to the dark haired man calmly and quietly explaining the correct technique of playing defense.

Turner is sweet with them….would you look at that.

I guess I expected him to be overbearing and strict. A hard-ass. But he's just the opposite. From this vantage point, there's hard evidence to believe that Jake Turner is a good man in disguise.

"Subject is not a total prick. I repeat, subject is not a

total prick. Rescues evil cats from trees and coaches young boys with a soft touch."

He skates backward, out of the way of the boys practicing, and blows his whistle. The boys line up, start taking shots on goal, and I start snapping pictures again.

He's graceful on those thin double blades. For a man his size, I didn't expect him to be so…elegant? Sensual? Erotic?

I guess the best way to describe him is erotic. Never thought I'd use that word to describe how someone skates but here you have it. Jake Turner is an erotic skater. Which obviously leads me to wonder what else he does this well.

Turner looks over his shoulder at me, and I automatically grin and wave because I'm a goober like that. He frowns, but I don't let it get me down. Not even a little.

"Nice try, pal. I'm on to you."

There's something deeply satisfying about discovering someone whom I thought was a self-centered ogre is actually a good person. Damn sure beats finding out the opposite.

While the boys carry on with their drills, Jake skates over to me and leans back against the railing to face the action.

"Any questions so far?"

"A million…" I say, examining his profile which is intense and laser focused on the kids. "how long have you been running this program?"

"About a year."

"Why? I mean, I know you sports stars have your pet causes, but why kids?"

He doesn't answer immediately. I get the impression he's deciding how much he wants to tell me. "I was these boys…someone helped me."

"Do you mind if I ask who?"

He looks over his shoulder and measures me. "The cop who caught me breaking into the high school. He played one year in the NHL. Ran a league for inner city kids."

I'm strangely both surprised and not surprised at all. If I've learned anything about him, it's to never rule anything out. "Why were you breaking into the school? Off the record."

He crosses his arms. "Boosting computers to pawn. Not a secret."

One of the boys skates up to us. He's got light brown shaggy hair sticking out from all sides of his helmet, a wide bright grin, and large hazel eyes with way too much trouble lurking there.

"This your girl, coach?" he says, with a half-cocked grin, overconfidence just oozing out of him. "She's cute."

You've gotta be kidding me. This kid doesn't look a day over thirteen.

"Show some respect, Kyle. Miss Anderson is a reporter for The Gazette."

Kyle's grin doesn't diminish one bit.

"Cool. You gonna write an article about us?"

"I am."

"Make sure you write something good about me, okay?" he says and skates away.

I see a successful career in law for Kyle should he ever wish it. Or politics.

"Why does he talk like a thirty-five-year-old player?"

Jake gives me a faint smile. "Foster care since he was five. Arrested for selling drugs when he was twelve." Any noticeable humor on Jake's face is gone. He's back to being shuttered and distant.

"He's seen more than most thirty-five-year-olds." Jake taps the railing. "Let me finish up with them and we can talk."

Then he skates back to the boys, leaving me alone—

and with more questions than I had when I arrived.

*　*　*

"What's that?"

Jakes raspy voice makes me jump in my seat. I was in the middle of blocking more Twitter trolls when he snuck up on me. I look up to find all six foot plus of him standing a few feet away in the aisle of the stands, glaring at my phone which I immediately turn off and stuff in my tote.

"Nothing…more blowback." I get no response to this, only more silence—his signature reaction. "What?"

"How bad is it?" He takes the seat right next to me and I immediately straighten my legs. Ever get a feeling that someone doesn't want to be touched? Yeah, that's what I'm getting from him.

"Pretty bad. Most of which I can't repeat."

"So delete your account."

"No. Absolutely not. Then they win. I won't be bullied into staying silent."

"It's Twitter. It's not real life."

I'm sure he's had his fair share of haters. "Is that why you aren't on social media?"

He turns to look at me. "Never had much use for it anyway. The team was handling my accounts until…"

He shrugs.

"How bad did it get for you?"

"I don't know. Never looked at the accounts."

"But?"

He smiles tightly. It's cold and lacking any humor. "I had to sell my townhouse in Boston. My neighbors couldn't take the press harassing them all the time."

That breaks my heart. Along with it comes a pang of guilt. I know something about the press and their thirst for a story. It can easily override common decency. "If you're not first, you're last," Ben used to say.

"I'm sorry."

He shrugs again. It's then, as I watch him absently stare out over the rink that I realize what it is about Turner that gives size and dimension to the dark cloud hanging over him. It's not lack of emotion. It's *too much* emotion.

It's grief.

"How do you do it? How do you keep going when everything falls apart?" he murmurs. "When you've screwed up so badly, there's no way to repair it?"

I'm not sure if he knows he's speaking out loud. That he's let his guard down when he's usually so buttoned up I can barely get a word out of him.

I don't have to guess what he's referring to, either. I can see the guilt on his face every day. Carrying the weight of someone's death on your shoulders must be exhausting.

"Everyone screws up, Jake. I've screwed up more times than I want to admit, but it's not going to stop me from trying again. I'm not going to go down without fighting for what I want." When all I get is silence, I glance sideways and study his profile. Elegant and proud. He seems a million miles away. "You know what tomorrow is?"

"What?" he says, humoring me.

"Tomorrow is another chance to get it right."

He takes a moment to look me over, his gaze sailing over my face. "What do you expect out of life, Anderson? Because I'm afraid you're gonna be sorely disappointed."

"Thanks for your dour two cents, Negative Nelly… And it's not what I expect. I don't expect anything."

A catalogue of emotions cross his face. "What do you want then?"

His genuine curiosity draws me in, makes me want to be honest with him…makes me willing.

"I want my life to be a grand adventure. I want to wake up in Tokyo and go to sleep in Rome. I want to live a life worth writing about. I want to worship and be worshipped…" Now that I've gotten started I can't seem to stop. "I want what my sister has, I want a once-in-a-lifetime love."

A slow, one-sided smile creeps up his handsome face. "Is that all?"

"It's a start…what about you?" I say, smiling back.

"What if I said I want all those things for you."

His unexpected answer sets me back. It makes me feel foolish, like he's teasing me again. "I'd say you're full of it."

Turner looks away, across the empty ice rink, his smile and the life in his eyes flickering dim. "I want to be left alone, Anderson. That's all I want."

Despite that he was just a world-class jerk, he sounds so defeated it troubles me.

Standing, he takes one last look at me and makes his way down the bleachers. I watch until he disappears into the tunnel. Making me wonder if maybe, just maybe, in some wild outlandish parallel universe, Jake Turner was being honest with me too.

* * *

Two days later I'm standing over the kitchen sink staring out the window and discover he's at it again. The shirtless wood chopping, that is. If he keeps it up, we'll have enough kindling to heat the house for the next decade. The view does hold a certain appeal, however. Especially since it's late in the afternoon and the sun is casting a golden, almost heavenly, glow on him.

I hate myself right now.

Absently, I turn on the faucet and the water sputters out. This is what the two hundred and fifty dollars I paid the plumber yesterday gets me.

"Not much to look at, but he's a gentleman."

Screeching, I wheel around to find Nan standing a few feet away, lazily petting Elvis. "Jesus. Can you keep the creeping to a minimum?"

Nan puts the cat down and Elvis sashays away, his tail at full mast. "My house, my rules," Nan's quick to remind me. "Means I can creep around as much as I want."

"Yeah, I know what it means." I grab the coffee beans out of the refrigerator, pour some in the speed grinder. "And I would hardly call him a gentleman," I feel compelled to shout over the loud buzzing. Once that's done, I spoon the fresh coffee grinds into the cappuccino machine, pull the lever, and wait for magic to happen.

A gentleman? Turner is a lot of things but a

gentleman isn't one of them. I'm still a little bruised over what happened at the rink. I thought we were getting somewhere. I thought we were sharing some deeply personal thoughts. And he turns around and ridicules me. What kind of person does that?

Cheap shots at my looks—those I know how to handle. But what he did cut much deeper.

"He's the opposite of that—whatever that is."

Except that he did save my life and is paying for my room. Can't forget that. Because fair is fair.

Then it hits me. My grandmother just took a swipe at Turner.

"I mean, he's not bad…looking, I mean." A bout of awkward silence follows in which I fetch some milk and pour it in my coffee. I don't know what just possessed me to come to his defense. God knows he doesn't deserve it.

"He's no beauty," Nan says. "You don't have to pretend for me. Now your dad, that's a good-looking man."

"You have told me *at least* a million times 'never trust a good-looking man.'"

"Well, that's true. But I'm talking about your dad, honey. That rule doesn't apply to him. Try and keep up, will you. Now where was I? Oh yes, the girls used to chase him." Nan's face tightens. "Including the hooker."

There she goes again. As much as I want to agree with her, I can't.

"Okay. First, I can't believe you're making me defend Zelda. Please stop calling her that. She is not a hooker."

"She sure acts like one."

"I see age hasn't taken the edge off. No, Nan. She doesn't—and for the record, Jake *is* a beauty."

Wtf am I saying? A beauty? I hate myself right now. "I mean…I don't think…I mean, objectively he's very handsome."

Nan frowns. "What are you saying, child? Spit it out."

"What I am saying, *grandmother*…" I can hear my voice rising as my frustration at this absurd discussion peaks. But the more I meditate on her disparaging remark, the more it gets under my skin. "Is that Jake is a very good-looking man. Objectively, he's probably the second-best looking man I've ever seen."

Fair is fair and Ben, the traitor, still takes first prize.

"Second-best, Carebear?" a scratchy voice inquires.

Every muscle in my body contracts involuntarily and not in a pleasant way. I can hear it distinctly—he's on the verge of outright laughter. Slowly, I turn to find Jake standing in the doorway, a smile flirting at the corners of his lips.

I hate myself right now. "Don't say another word."

Marching over to the pantry, I retrieve the monkey wrench from the portable tool box and open the doors under the sink. I need to hide my face right now and under the sink seems to be the perfect place.

Laying down on my back, I cram my head under the sink and inspect the pipes. Do I know anything about pipes? Hell no. But apparently neither does the plumber I hired.

"Don't break anything," Nan calls out.

"Thank you for your vote of confidence," I return.

"I'm confident you know nothing about plumbing, sweetheart."

Whatever. From my spot on the ground, I can see Turner's boots. He hasn't moved, as I had hoped.

"Go away Turner. You're killing my focus."

"Yeah, I know. I'm the second most handsome man you've ever seen."

Ugh. Wonderful. He's going to milk this for all it's worth.

A beat later he's on the ground next to me,

attempting to inject his massive upper body into the small space along mine.

"What are you doing?"

"Making sure you don't break anything I can't fix."

"Nobody asked you. I've got it, but thanks."

"Move out. I can't breathe under here with you flapping your lips."

Jerk. My blood pressure hits a dangerous level. The last thing I need right now is to look incompetent in front of this guy, giving him more material to ridicule me with. "I'll do no such thing."

"What's the problem with the sink?" he says ignoring my attempt to maintain control over the situation.

"It's still sputtering. And I just handed Spalding two fifty to fix it."

Turner wraps his fingers around the handle of the monkey wrench over mine and an electric current travels up my arm. I hate that phrase, but in this case, an electric current is the only way to describe the feeling.

Then he levels me with an unblinking stare that could arguably make a grown man cry. Not me. Na-ha. Nope. I've seen this fraud in action with the kids. Scowl away, pal. I've got your number.

"Let go Anderson."

Let's keep it real, though. Nan is right. I hand over the wrench because who am I kidding? I know less than nothing about plumbing.

Turner gets his game face on while I watch him scope out the pipes. "Sputtering you said?"

"Hmm."

He checks the tightness on the washers while I watch. "Do you know anything about plumbing, or do I have to call Spalding and drag his ass?"

"Where I grew up, you had to know how to do a little bit of everything."

I did more research on him last night and discovered there's very little out there about him. "In Chicago, right?"

"Yeah."

"Why did you have to know a little bit of everything?" I can't help it, asking questions is a compulsion.

Turner pauses his fiddling with the washers and meets my eyes. "What, you didn't Google me?" A one-sided smirk shapes his lips. "I thought you were a reporter."

My blood boils, needling the skin on my neck. "Look, I don't really care that your delicate feelings were hurt by some big bad journalist in the past. But taking shots at me won't make that go away. I was asking you because I don't always believe everything I read."

The smirk drops and a small part of me feels vindicated. I'm fairly certain he seldom gets called out on his shitty behavior and it's about time someone did.

"South side," he says and resumes tinkering with the pipes. "Public housing doesn't have good plumbing so I learned to fix things."

"You lived there with your parents?" I prompt. I found almost nothing about his family online, and my mouth is a runaway train right now. When something piques my interest nothing can stop it, and Jake Turner definitely piques my interest.

He doesn't answer right away. I can practically feel him internally debating how much to tell me. "My mom…until I was fourteen. Then foster care."

That explains a lot.

"Let's see if that worked," he says, scooting out from under the sink.

He stands, offering me a hand up, and when I place mine in his, the feeling returns. It wasn't a fluke or my imagination. A sense of awareness covers every inch of my skin. And it's not a cold feeling. Just the opposite, it's warm and soothing, drawing me in. Something strange is happening here.

"You two gonna stand there all day holding hands, or are you going to help me make dinner?"

Nan's voice is nails on a chalkboard. We break apart and he turns to face her. "Thanks, Martha, but I've got plans."

Then he walks out the back door without saying goodbye while I stare after him.

"How's the faucet?" Nan asks.

I turn it on, and a steady stream of water flows out. "Fixed."

Chapter Ten

"Finally! I was beginning to wonder if I had to come drag you out," Gina says as soon as I push through the stack of bodies to reach the bar she's standing behind.

Queen is lit. I can barely breathe in here it's so packed, and this place has a high exposed ceiling.

"Yeah, I know," I mutter sheepishly. "Sorry it took so long for me to put this on." I open my (Jackie's) leather jacket and flash her my vintage Superman T-shirt beneath.

"You—" she says, pointing to a twenty something hipster with blond dreads. "—out of that barstool. This is the VIP section by order of the owner."

Hipster kid makes a face. "Fuck that, I spend money here. Lemme talk to him."

Not the answer Gina was looking for. One well-groomed eyebrow twitches up.

"Hey, crystal deodorant. You're looking at her. So get up, or I'll have Dana escort you out." She hooks a thumb at the dude at the front door. Dana happens to be a seven foot Samoan. Sensing the attention, he dips his chin at us. One glance at Dana and the hipster kid slides off the stool.

"Haha. That has to be the most satisfying."

"The mostest," she echoes.

If you had any idea how many times we were bullied to either move over, or move altogether off the bleachers at football games back in high school you would understand.

Grabbing a glass from a stack behind her, she lifts it. "What's your poison?"

"I don't really have one so you decide. Nothing too sweet or strong though. I'm walking home."

Gina gets busy mixing ingredients, smashing mint, and pouring the contents of the shaker in a tumbler. I take a sip and smile. Just perfect.

"Mojito, but with my own little twist. Raspberry infusion."

"Deeeelicious."

She leans her elbows on the bar, a big toothy smile on her face. "Can you believe this is us?"

"Speak for yourself. And yes, I can believe this is you. You were never one to back down. Me, on the other hand…"

"Everyone can't be a fighter. You're strong in your own way…what you did took some guts."

"Or sheer stupidity." I shrug, sucking down my drink. "May I have another please?"

"You sure? That went down a little quickly."

"You're right. Maybe I shouldn't." Snapshots of all the things that have taken a turn for the worse the last few months flips through my mind. "Maybe I should."

Two hours later…

"I dunno. I dunno. Maybe it was for the best. He was a lousy kisser, know what I mean?" I can hear myself, and yet I don't seem to be in charge of my mouth. "Like swallowin' a chuncka raw tuna. Like bad sushi."

"He sounds wonderful," Gina deadpans.

"I should get going."

"Tough love?"

"Shoot."

"You're the biggest lightweight. Those mojitos weren't strong at all."

"Not a drinker. Shouda told you that."

Gina slides a glass of water in front of me. "Drink up and I'll drive you home."

"No…no, no. I'll call my dad to come get me. Gene missed out on all that good stuff when I was in high school. He's got a lot of catching up to do."

I take out my phone, hold it up, and hit my dad's cell icon.

"Hello? Carrie?"

Why does he sound winded? I shove the strange thought aside because somewhere in the recesses of my mind I know that I am mildly inebriated and shouldn't attempt to think right now.

"Why do you sound winded, Dad? Never mind. Can you pick me up? I'm at Gina's—'scuse me—Regina's bar. It's beautiful and it's called Queen. Cause she's a beautiful queen…"

Chuckling, Gina helps the bar back clear the counter of empty bottles and glasses.

"I'm…" Dad exhales. "Yeah, okay. Give me a few minutes."

"Everything alright?" she says, reading the puzzled look on her face.

I shake off the strange feeling. Now is not the time to play investigative reporter. "Yeah…he should be here soon."

Ten minutes later my investigative alarm starts ringing when I see Jake walk in the door, scan the room, and make a beeline for me.

"Hello, stud muffin," I hear coming from my long lost friend. "Damn, he's fine."

"Not my type," I hear myself retort. Which of course is a bald-faced lie. Whether he's my type or not doesn't mean jack. The inconvenient truth is that I am one hundred percent attracted to a man I can barely tolerate, and who can tolerate me even less.

"Smoking hot and built like a brick shit house isn't your type?"

"Not this time. Also, he's an insufferable stick in the mud."

"So you know him well?"

"Not at all."

Which is mostly the truth. Turner is close to impossible to pin down. One minutes he's gazing at me like he wants to discover every single one of my secrets, and the next he wants to shove me in a box under the bed.

Speaking of moods, Turner walks up with his usual permanent stamp of disapproval on his face. "You need a ride home?"

"Huh?"

"A ride."

"Where's Gene?" I look around him, attempting to

get a gander at the door.

"He's…he asked me to come get you. He's indisposed."

"Indiswhat?"

Sighing, Turner slides onto the empty stool next to mine. "Club soda please," he asks the young male bartender who scurries over with a look of unadulterated hero worship on his face.

Most of the time, I forget that Turner is a world class famous athlete. That he has fans. i.e. people that don't know his personality is rough with a capital R.

"Regina Polizzi meet Jake Turner. Turner meet the owner of this fine establishment and my only friend."

Grinning, Regina takes Jake's outstretched hand. "I know who you are."

Turner—he doesn't smile. God forbid the man appear pleasant. Too much work.

"You'll have to excuse him, G. Turner has a permanent case of the sadz. But he did save my life. He did do that. Probably regrets it now. Don't cha, Turner? Don't you wish you left me out there to become a human popsicle?"

"No."

"That's it. That's all you have to say?"

"No. I don't regret saving you from becoming a human popsicle."

My attention swings back to Gina. She's watching us closely, a smile pulling up one corner of her mouth.

"Isn't he a hoot?"

Jake's elbow bushes against mine and a sense of awareness zings up my arm.

My gaze flickers over him as I drink my water. The thin black sweater he's wearing skims the swell of his chest. He trimmed his hair. It's in one of those side parts now, in the same style every other pro athlete on the planet wears. But damn it looks good on him.

My eyes can't seem to stay away. They're bad, with no regard for manners whatsoever. In fact, I'm studying him so intensely I could get a PhD in his anatomy. While that goes on, my insides do that thing that I'm pretty sure they should not be doing about this man in particular. They flip out.

I don't like myself very much right now.

Regina places her hands on the bar and leans in. "Hey, you know what I was going to ask you…are you dating anyone? Because Luca is back in town and he's single again."

Of course he's single again. Luca is single every three

months like clockwork. Regina's middle brother is a total player. I would rather eat bad sushi.

"No…no, I…" How do I say this without insulting her brother. "We never had…any chemistry."

It's a total lie and Regina knows it. Last time Luca saw me I was seventeen. Back then, he wouldn't have looked at me twice even if I was on fire.

Someone down the other end of the bar waves to Gina, a guy wearing a suit. "I'll be just a minute, Care."

"Take your time," I tell her even though I don't want to be alone with Turner longer than necessary. I've got a nice buzz going and I'd like to keep it that way.

"Like we have," comes from my immediate right.

This requires my immediate attention. I glance over, and find him staring back at me. "Come again?"

Because I know I'm still tipsy and couldn't have heard him correctly.

"Chemistry. You know, that thing between us."

I scratch my temple. Maybe I'm drunker than I realize. "Chemistry?"

"Yeah."

I'm confused. "You think we have chemistry?"

Dead serious, he nods. What do *I* do? I look around. This can't be real. I look over his head. In the opposite direction. Either I'm in a fever dream or someone is punking me.

"Stop messing around. And where the hell is Gene?"

"Busy…" Turner's gaze falls to my lips. "Tell me you don't feel it."

Wtf?

My pulse jumps. "We don't have chemistry." I can't look at him as I say it though. I can't keep the truth out of my eyes. I can't do it drunk or sober. He's got me completely boxed in.

Down the bar, Regina is directing her staff. She probably found our constant bickering boring. I can't blame her.

Dark sapphire eyes hold mine for what feels like forever. So does the slow progress of heat marching up my neck. It's not chemistry. It's a sickness, this attraction.

"Anymore chemistry and we'd burn down the house if we ever slept together."

Instantly, I picture him naked, and my cheeks burn red hot.

He leans in. "You're thinking about it now, aren't you…"

What has gotten into him?

"No. And the Lake Placid Fire Department can tuck

in because it's never gonna happen."

Silence follows. So does a staring contest as per our usual routine. One...two...three beats later...

"We'll see." Sliding off the stool, he motions to the door. "Come on. It's late and it looks like your friend needs to close up."

I say goodbye to Gina spending a good ten minutes of that time insisting I pay for the drinks and her insisting she won't let me. Then I follow Turner to the Expedition parked outside. He opens the door for me, and I slide in. Before he shuts it, however, he hangs on for a while.

"Second-best, huh?" There's a spark in his eyes tonight I haven't seen before. It makes him ten times more attractive. This is bad news for me.

"Hard to believe you're even on the list at all—I know. Then again, I haven't gotten out much lately."

He shuts the door and the dark chuckle tails him to the driver's side. He gets in and starts the engine. In the quiet of the dark cab, the smell of fresh oil paint and turpentine hits me. It reminds me of the farmhouse. It seems like an eternity ago instead of two months.

Glancing at the back seat, I spot three canvases covered in cheese cloth.

"When did you learn how to paint? I mean, I know you're a pretty good hockey player, but you're an amazing artist."

The booze is hitting me hard, my eyelids getting heavy, my lips loose. Add to it the cozy comfort of the SUV, and the familiar scent of the man seated next to me and I'm super relaxed. For the first time since we've met we are on a level playing field. "I mean it, Turner. Your paintings are…they take my breath away."

Every time I pass by the ones hanging in the main house I have to stop and stare. There's something about them that feeds the soul, soothes it in the same way a great piece of music does. It's more than skill. It's the emotion he pours into them. And if Jake Turner does everything else with as much passion and attention, I shudder to think.

Smoothly, he pulls the Expedition onto the mostly deserted road and drives up the hill that leads to the Cottages.

He clears his throat, and I glance over. One hand is on the steering wheel, the other strokes his chin. "My therapist. She wanted me to journal or something—after the accident."

I twist in my seat to watch him, to see if there's an

actual crack in the ice, but he's stoic as always.

"I used to draw when I was a kid…One thing led to another. I taught myself how to use oils…"

He shrugs, a tight sheepish smile shaping his lips. Warmth spreads in my chest. It's really kind of pathetic how high I feel simply because he chose to share this piece of himself with me.

"You're incredibly talented."

The veins in his neck pop. His chest rises and falls. His body reacting while his mouth stays still. He doesn't know what to do with the compliment.

"It's okay, Turner. Don't worry. I won't think highly of you if that's what you're worried about."

It's enough to set him at ease, his big body sinking into the leather set.

A few minutes later, he parks the SUV in front of the cottages and turns off the engine. I'm too tired to do anything else other than breathe. Jake opens my door, unbuckles the seat belt, and picks me up. Scoops me into his arms again like he did the fateful night at the farmhouse when he saved my life. Good old Jake is always there when you need him.

Every instinct in my body forces me to wrap my arms around his neck and place my head where it meets his shoulder. I take a deep breath, inhaling his skin, scratch my fingers through the hair at the back of his head. I can't stop touching him.

He makes a sound, and I do it again. I'm so tired I can't even be bothered to care that I'm being inappropriate.

Pushing my door open, he carries me inside and gently places me on the bed. Only I don't let go. Nope. I hang onto his neck like a baby monkey.

"Thanks, Turner. That…that was nice of you."

He studies me closely. His intense gaze flicking between my lips and my eyes. For a second, I get the impression he's going to do it, he's finally going to kiss me, and my body comes awake, prepared for anything. It's been so long I'll probably screw it up, but at least I'll have fun trying. But right before I take a victory lap, he pulls back and breaks the weak hold I have on him.

"Night, Carebear."

And then he's gone, locking the door as he leaves.

Chapter Eleven

"Where are the flowers?" Dad shouts over the din of nearly two dozen people working furiously to set up the main dining room for a wedding party of seventy-five people.

It's the day of the Azzeritti Comofort wedding and every single person on staff is working today.

May weddings are notoriously unpredictable around here. We've learned over the years to have both indoor and outdoor seating available should a freak snowstorm or spring shower roll in, but it looks like the bride is in luck today. I'd like to believe that the clear blue sky spotted with white puffs of clouds up above is a good omen for the rest of her marriage.

It's also unusually warm. Warm enough that I'm wearing my sister's Chloe peacock blue minidress with a ruffle collar. It's safe to say Jackie is never getting this one back.

"Calling the florist again right now," Nan yells back.

You know it's all hands on deck if Nan has been

enlisted to pitch in. Elvis jumps up on one of the tables and I almost scream. It's taken me hours to make sure each tablecloth is pristine.

Nan grabs him and pats the fat bastard's head before she drops him.

My job is to steam linens and set the tables. Which I've been doing since 7 am this morning. Nan catches me yawning for the third time and makes a face.

"Go get some coffee and I'll finish the steaming."

"I'm fine. I only have a few runners left to do," I tell her as I lay out the pale sage cloth down one of the long banquet tables.

I'm not fine. I'm exhausted. Writer's block is a bitch.

I must have started and scrapped the article on Jake and the hockey program five times in the last four days. Something about it didn't seem right. It sounded stiff and boring. In other words, like hard news. And that's not what Hal asked for. So late last night, I started over.

After staring at the computer screen for a solid hour and a half, I just began typing. I don't know, maybe it was the combination of too much caffeine and mixed emotions, but my fingers started moving and didn't stop till dawn. It's finally done. And before I second guess myself for the fifth time, I plan on emailing it to him tomorrow.

I haven't seen Jake since the night he drove me home from Gina's place four days ago. Since the near kiss, as I like to call it. Since the night he opened the door a little more and let me in. The same night he said the quiet words out loud.

He thinks we have *chemistry*.

I wasn't sure whether to believe my ears, but frankly it's a relief to know I'm not the only one feeling it for once. I'm so used to pining from afar I have no idea how to behave when it's reciprocated.

Where that leaves us—I don't know. Or takes us, for that matter. But I'm more than willing to find out. And hey, it's not like I'm getting ahead of myself. I know this is a temporary thing. Everyone needs human touch once in a while. I'm not deluding myself into thinking I'm the girl of his dreams. Maybe he's just as lonely as I am. Everybody needs somebody sometime, right?

"They're here!" Nan exclaims seeing the delivery truck pull up to the service entrance. Once the flowers are schlepped inside, we finish setting up.

Two hours later the wedding party begins to trickle in. One by one, they take a seat in one of the white Chippendale chairs on the flagstone patio. The nondenominational ceremony will be held outside overlooking the lake, under an arch made of white birch branches adorned with white flowers.

While the last of the guests arrive and take their seats, the minister takes her place on the altar.

Meanwhile, I hang back, leaning against the side of the house to watch. The backyard slopes down all the way to the lake's edge so it's a bird's eye view from this angle.

The music starts and the groom comes down the aisle, shaking hands with guests, a goofy smile plastered on his boyish face. His expression when he finally steps on stage says it all. It's the face of a man in love, more than happy to be getting married today.

I can't help but wonder if there's a man out there, somewhere, that will look like that for me one day. Call me a hopeless romantic, but I sure hope so.

The best man turns and a pang of recognition hits me. It takes me a moment to pin point why he looks familiar. His face is more angular. He's shed about fifty pounds and added a lot of muscle, but the eyes are the same. It's someone in my graduating class. Sean Gordon or something, I think.

He seems to be having a good time, joking around

with the groomsmen. Until the music starts. Then they all sober up and face the French doors, waiting for the bride to appear.

When she finally emerges, led by three bridesmaids and two adorable flower girls, the guests turn in their seats to watch, faces lighting up as she comes down the aisle escorted by her very proud father. The crowd claps and cheers. A few even whistle, making me laugh. I've never seen such a rowdy wedding ceremony.

Meanwhile, the bride is unconventionally beautiful. Willowy, ethereal, a woodland pixie with short dark hair and an easy smile. No veil, her hair is decorated with a wreathe of vines and white flowers, her dress is a flowing mass of white chiffon. And she's obviously incandescently in love with her groom judging by the way she's looking at him. Her father hands her over to the man she's about to marry and the ceremony begins.

I don't know what it is about this wedding, but I am swept away by the raw emotion emanating from the crowd and the couple. This is the stuff of legends and fairytales. This is what my sister has, what I aspire to. Unchecked, a tear escapes down my cheek and I wipe it away. There's no lonelier feeling than being around true love.

The ceremony starts and soon enough it's time for the vows, which the couple has written.

"I never believed in love at first bite until your dog chased me down the street and took a chunk out of my calf. Dexter's no longer with us, but I have to believe it was all part of his grand plan to bring us together," the groom starts. "Thanks, Dex. I forgive you for the eight stitches." The crowd laughs. "Since then, you've given me seven of the best years of my life, Amy…" Taking a deep breath, tears begin to fall down his face. The bride, tears in her eyes too, reaches out and wipes them away for him. And in turn, he kisses her palm.

"Loving you has made me stronger, kinder, wiser, and more patient," he continues, voice shaking. "You've taught me that love is bigger than time and space, more powerful than cancer, and more enduring than anything in this world. And whatever we face, whatever life has in store for us, I vow to make you laugh when you feel crappy. I vow never to hold it against you when you yell at me about leaving the wet towel on the carpet. And I vow to take every step of this journey with you as long as I live."

* * *

"Ladies room?" one of the wedding guests asks me.

It snaps me out of spell. "Down the hall on your right," I inform her with a smile.

Physically and emotionally drained, I yawn again and lean against the wall at the edge of the room for support. There wasn't a dry eye in the house after the bride finished her vows. Even Nan, hiding in the wings, looked on the verge of crying.

From what I've been able to gather from eavesdropping on some private whisperings is that the bride has been battling cancer on and off for the last three years, and she's in remission now. Here I am, feeling sorry for myself when other people are really suffering. It's a stark reminder to be grateful and count my blessings.

The band is playing a horrible cover of *Celebrate!* Somewhere Kool and the Gang is cringing. The bride and groom don't seem to mind though. They slow dance while chaos reigns around them.

"Where can I get a drain snake?"

I look over my shoulder and find Jake standing close enough to touch. Seeing him makes my breath catch. This is not a good sign. I am way too into him already for this to end anyway other than badly for me.

He's in his painting clothes. An old Henley shirt

streaked with color, his gray sweatpants, and Timberlands. The only addition is a beat-up Bears ball cap with the rim pulled low.

He looks me over, his open gaze roaming down my bare legs to my high heeled booties and back up to my face.

"You look nice."

My face nearly splits in two by the sheer force of the smile that compliment elicits. "What do you need a drain snake for?"

"Shower."

"I can send one of the guys—"

He shakes his head while his gaze remains on my mouth. "No. I'll do it."

I've learned not to waste my energy arguing with this man and motion him out of the room and into the hallway.

We get only a few feet when I spot Sean coming from the opposite direction. His eyes narrow on me, rake up and down my body. Surprise grows on his face.

"Pizza Face?" he nearly shouts, grinning widely.

My heart stops. For a single solitary suspended moment, it stops beating in shock and shame. Then it races ahead. I honestly never anticipated hearing that name ever again.

My feet follow suit, abruptly halting in the middle of the hallway. Jake almost runs me over. He comes just short of it by bracing onto my shoulders. Then he backs off. Way off, it feels like. Because a cold chill runs up my spine, the absence of his body heat noticeable.

This is it. This is what I've been dreading all along and it's happening in front of the one person I want to impress, the one who thinks *I look nice*, the one man that thinks *we have chemistry*.

I'm finally close to getting the boy I want. I can't be Pizza Face in front of Jake.

While Sean walks up to us, I am paralyzed with fear. I can't even look over my shoulder to gauge what's going on with him. I'm not strong enough for that right now.

"It's really you—holy shit," the insensitive asshole keeps repeating. "Sean? Gorman?" Like I should be excited to see him. We were strangers. Sean was just someone in my class that ignored me ninety-nine percent of the time unless someone was making fun of me.

"I know, I know. I look different too. Lost a few pounds..." he continues, mistaking my silence. He looks around. "You work here?"

Years of self-discipline kick in. I force the words out,

taking care to deliver them in a steady and measured way. "My family owns it…yes, I work here."

I hear myself sound indifferent and cool when in reality I'm falling apart inside.

"You look great. Damn, I barely recognized you, girl."

I want to puke.

While Sean slow nods and undresses me with his eyes, a low growl comes from somewhere behind me. Unfortunately for me, Jake didn't cut and run. He heard everything.

Sean's attention darts over my shoulder. I know the moment he recognizes Jake by the look of surprise. "Aren't you Jake Turner?"

Jake makes a humming noise. He steps closer, his body brushing up against my arm and hip. Even under layers of clothes, everywhere we touch a prickle of awareness fans out.

"What are you doing here, dude?" Sean examines Jake's clothes. "You're not here for the wedding obviously. Hey man, can I get an autograph?"

"Fuck, no," Jake fires back. "And stop looking at my girl like she's a snack or I'll break you in two."

Ummm…

Sean takes a step back, hands raised. He chuckles darkly. "No disrespect, bro. She and I go way back."

"No, we don't," I blurt out, angry at his insinuation.

Sean gives me a dirty half-cocked grin. "Whatever…"

He doesn't remember my name. I can see it in his eyes.

Sean back peddles out of the hallway and disappears into the dining room from the doorway on the other side.

And all I can think as I watch him go is…my one true test and I failed.

* * *

There's something to be said for pride. I've been told it's a sin. That it cometh before the falleth or some such nonsense. But I disagree. Right now the only thing holding me together is the last bit of pride I possess. If it weren't for pride, I would be falling to pieces right now.

"Who was that?"

Swallowing the lump in my throat, I ignore Jake's question and take off down the hallway at a brisk pace.

"Carrie," comes from right behind me.

"Stay here and I'll bring it to you."

"The hell I will. Who was he?"

It figures that the one time I don't want to talk, he's feeling chatty.

"No one. Leave me alone, Turner."

Bursting through the double-doors of the kitchen—the kitchen on the family side of the building; not the hotel kitchen—I head straight for the walk-in pantry. Even though it's dark, I don't turn on the light. Right now I need a dark hole to get lost in and catch my breath. My hands are shaking and my legs feel like jelly from the aftermath of the adrenaline rush.

Unfortunately for me, Turner is still in hot pursuit. "Carrie?"

Chalk it up to being tired and drained from the beautiful wedding I just witnessed, but I'm beginning to crack. No matter how hard I try to keep a lid on it, my chin starts to shake. Mostly because I'm mad at myself. I thought I'd come so far only to be reminded that one word had the power to wipe away a decade of hard work.

"Carrie…" Jake's outline takes up the entire doorway. Backlit, he looks more ominous than usual.

I shrink even further into the pantry and don't stop until my back hits the shelves and the mason jars ring. I press the tips of my fingers into the corners of my eyes to stave off the tears. "I don't wanna talk," I say sharply and pray he gets the message.

For a moment it looks like he's about to leave, but then he stops. "You're upset. Who was that guy?"

If I was thinking straight, I would be the one asking questions. Like…what possessed him to tell Sean I was his girl. That—I would be interested in hearing more about. As it stands however, I'm barely capable of not crying.

"Just a guy from high school…a nobody." Then I recall and the humiliation hits me all over again. I was the nobody. Not Sean. I was the one.

"Did you date him?" He almost sounds upset.

"He didn't even know my name, Jake. No, we did not date. We never even spoke once before today."

One slow step at a time, Jake comes closer. Close enough that we're both in the shadows. I can barely see the outline of his features at this point.

Taking his ball cap off, he rakes his fingers through his hair and sighs, then he stuffs the hat in the waistband of his sweatpants. "Why did he call you that name?"

His voice is quiet and gentle, but it only makes me feel worse because it sounds like pity to me. It's more than I can handle and the pressure cooker explodes. My eyes fill with water and empty, tears pouring down my face.

I purposely didn't Google search any of his past girlfriends because it would've completely intimidated me. And now he expects me to expose the most painful aspects of my life, the ones I have tried so desperately to put behind me.

"You can tell me."

That catapults me into rage and frustration. "What the hell do you want me to say, Jake? That he called me Pizza Face because I had really bad acne for most of my life? Do you really want to hear about that? Does it satisfy your curiosity to hear that I was unpopular and unattractive. That nobody could ever remember my name because they were so used to calling me Pizza Face? That all I did throughout high school is dream about getting out of this fucking dog year town where one year feels like forever only to come back broke and unemployed. There, I said it. You win! I'm a loser. Happy now?"

I am crying so hard at this point that I swallow a hiccup.

"Fucking hell," he mutters, and suddenly reaches out, cupping his warm hands around my face.

Operating on instinct more than anything else, I automatically reach up and take hold of his wrists. All my senses sharpen. I can feel his pulse under my thumb, the rhythm of his breath against my chest as he draws me closer. The scent of soap and shampoo and turpentine.

He wraps me up in his arms and holds on so tightly I can hardly breathe. And still, I can't stop crying, my body shaking from all the emotion pouring out of me. It's been pent up for so long, now that it's been set loose it doesn't want to abate.

"I'm sorry," he whispers in my ear and plants a kiss on the side of my face. That's all it takes. Just that one simple soft kiss is enough to make my legs weak. "I didn't mean to push. I take it back. I'll do anything for you to stop crying…"

In my heels, our bodies line up perfectly. Pelvises kissing, my curves buffering the hard planes of his muscles. I'm surrounded by heat and comfort the likes of which I've never felt before. But what sucks the most is that now that I know how wonderful it feels, I'm afraid of how I will ever do without it.

"I didn't mean to make you feel worse. I…I didn't know…I…"

"It's okay," I murmur into his chest. The tears have stopped, leaving me more drained than ever. "I'm just really mad at myself. I thought I was over this place and all the baggage that comes with it."

"I swore to myself that I would never make you cry again."

It takes me a minute to press rewind and search our history. Then I recall the press badge.

"The farmhouse?"

"Yeah."

A warm hand brushes up and down my back and every nerve ending on my body comes alive. "It feels like a million years ago…"

He makes a humming sound and the vibration travels from his chest to mine, my nipples hardening. If I was halfway to being turned on before, I'm all the way there now.

"I thought you saved me so you could make beef jerky out of me."

One…two…three seconds of silence.

"What?" Then he starts chuckling. No actual sound comes out of him. It's the soft shaking of his chest that tips me off. Squeezing me tighter, he says, "That explains a lot."

He exhales sharply, his hands moving up my back and over my shoulders. They brush along my neck, and I shiver in pleasure. I could die from pleasure right now and he hasn't even touched the good parts yet.

Holding my face, guided by nothing other than touch, he brushes my cheeks with his thumbs. His breath fans my face, and I hear him murmur, "Carebear…"

His lips brush over mine and pull back. It's basically a tease. And nowhere near enough. This thing between us has been stoked to a fever pitch and one small chaste kiss is not going to cut it.

Standing on my toes, I abandon any doubts or sense of inadequacy and kiss him back. I dig my fingers in his henley and tug him closer, and he doesn't need any more help after that. He slams me into the shelves, pins my hips down with his, and makes me feel how hard he is. Those sweatpants don't leave anything to the imagination. I moan into his mouth and he takes it, kissing me with everything he's been holding back.

Holy hell, Jake was right. If we ever do sleep together we *will* burn the house down. Better make sure it's not on a holiday when the fire department is on a skeleton crew.

"Elvis. Elvis…where the hell is that cat. Elvis!"

Both of us freeze. Hot breaths mingling. I reach up and cover his mouth with my hand. He pressed the head of his erection into me, and I take the hand and cover my mouth with it instead.

"Is somebody here?"

"No," I answer automatically.

"Okay."

"I'll be out in a minute."

"Good. The wedding guests are leaving," Nan answers. "And bring Jake with you."

Chapter Twelve

"*Musing of a High School Loser,*" Hal reads the title of my column out loud, grinning from ear to ear. "Terrific. I loved it."

Seeing his genuine reaction, I finally take a deep breath. We're meeting in his office today to discuss the article, and I've been in a cold sweat until his very minute.

"Even better than I expected," he says staring down at a printed copy.

"Really? You're not just saying that, right? Because I wrote this at 4 a.m. high on Monster drinks and peanuts."

"It's funny, sweet, irreverent. This Kyle kid is really something special…" Glancing up, he takes his glasses off and laces his fingers together on the desk. "I think if you and Gray put your heads together and promote it on social media you're going to earn quite a local following."

Now it's my turn to grin from ear to ear.

"I'm prepared to offer you a regular spot, your own column, if you think you can sustain the quality."

There's no question I can—but how can the paper afford it?

"What about the paper's finances?"

"You write the articles. Let me worry about the money. Been doing it all my life. I'll come up with something."

Everything goes so well with Hal, on my way out, I invite Gray for coffee. I've been away from the Lakes for so long, he's more likely to know what's new and hot on the fringe, what's on the come-up, than I would. Maybe he can point me in the right direction on where to look.

"So, Gray, you have a girlfriend?" I ask after we discussed that he wants to focus exclusively on online sports media. It seems everyone in his generation wants to be the next Barstool Sports. "A boyfriend? Both?"

His full lips kick up on one side. "Neither."

"Why do I feel like I'm not getting the whole story?"

"Reporters, man…" he says shaking his head, a big grin spreading across his boyish face.

His dark brown gaze drops to the dark wood tabletop. He rolls the empty take-out cup between his hands. "There is someone I'm interested in…but…she's not interested in me."

"Now we're getting somewhere. How do you know?"

"How do I know what? That I like her?" He makes a face. "I know. Trust me, I know."

I can't help but laugh. What a terrible job of acting coy. He's more than interested. He has a major thing for someone.

"Does she actually know you like her?"

"Like…have I asked her out?"

"Yeah, Gray. Dating. I know you're only twenty-two, but tell me you've dated before."

In a lot of ways he reminds me of me at that age. I was just starting to figure it out as well. Unsure of myself but willing to try only to backpedal later when the opportunity presented itself.

"Yeah…I mean, not a lot. Some." He fidgets in his seat. "A few times."

"Let me give you a little advice," I say, leaning forward conspiratorially. "God knows I'm no expert on dating myself, but I do know something about women having been one since birth…"

I have his complete attention. Unblinking, he stares at me as if jewels are about to drip from my lips.

"Women are attracted to confidence. It doesn't matter

<u>how old, tall, rich, or handsome you are. If you can sell the confidence without being cheesy or gross, you'll get the girl eventually.</u>

"I'm not saying bravado. That's not it. I'm saying the confidence that comes from believing in yourself. From within. You believe and other people will begin to agree with you…and when your chance comes, make sure you take it."

"Confidence…" he murmurs, his gaze directed out the cafe window and faraway. Then he snaps out of it. "Let's post your column on Facebook and Twitter."

* * *

"Why the face, kid?" Nan asks from her chair near the fireplace, her trusty feline companion at her feet.

She's working on her needlepoint. Comfort Cottages is famous for it. The hotel has been selling her signature needlepoint trimmed pillows and duvets for decades. And making a tidy profit too. When I saw the balance sheet, I thought it was a typo.

I'm restless and grouchy and I can't seem to find anything to hold my interest. Presently, I started and DNFed two books and started and scraped a new column. Unlike Elvis who has an unhealthy interest in his privates.

"Elvis is licking his balls again."

"Everyone should have a hobby," Nan replies without missing a beat.

I came home from my coffee date with Gray to find out Jake went out of town without a word. Maybe that has something to do with it. But it's not like he owes me an explanation. I have no right to be bruised about it. We shared a couple of kisses. Big deal. Were they fantastic kisses? Definitely. The best I've ever had? You bet.

And still that means nothing. I'm a big girl now, playing by big girl rules. And the rules of courtship these days are no one owes anyone anything. Double that sentiment if the person in question is a super famous sports star. One with a star a touch tarnished, but a star nonetheless.

"Did Jake say where he was going?"

I give her a look. "Nan….we're not talking about Jake."

"So he *didn't* tell you."

Leave it to my grandmother to pour salt on a wound and kick it across the room.

"No. We're barely friends. He doesn't have to explain himself or tell me when he leaves town."

"Is that what you kids call it these days?"

I glance back up at her and find her rapt attention on her needlepoint, a soft smile of her face.

"It's pointless anyway…I'm going back to California as soon as possible. This place…is not for me."

"Bullshit."

"Nan."

"A place is what you make of it."

"I'm going out," Dad announces, stepping into the doorway dressed and shaved.

It's eight. My father is usually sleeping in his chair in front of the TV by this hour.

"Out?" I feel the need to affirm. "As in, out with company?"

"Meeting the guys for a beer."

"Have fun," Nan chirps and we both turn to get a better look at her. Very odd.

Dad gives me a *beats me too* look and waves.

By nine, I crawl into bed, defeated. No Jake. No friends. Even Gene is out. My father has a better social life than I do. I did not see my life going this way. For half a second, I contemplate going to Regina's but she's likely busy working and I'm not going to be the sad chick at the end of the bar nursing a soda for three hours. I refuse to be that girl in this story.

I do the next best thing, I call my sister to complain. "He didn't say a word. Just mauled me in the pantry and left the next day."

"How big is he?"

Pregnancy has turned my mild-mannered sister into a gutter rat. "Are you serious?"

"Why wouldn't I be?"

"You expect me to tell you how big the guy I have an unhealthy crush on is?"

"What's the big deal. You want me to tell you how big Charlie is?"

"No! Don't ever have another kid. Pregnancy is turning you into a crazy person."

"Oh, Charlie's home. Time for sex. Love you."

After Jackie hangs up on me, I'm still not tired so like the high school loser I am, I Google him…again.

A YouTube video of his last Stanley Cup win pops up and I press play. On skates, Jake is poetry in motion. Fast, graceful. Erotic. The change in him is so obvious now. Watching him play with so much unbridled energy, so many emotions crossing his face, he barely looks like the same person. It makes me sad, actually. I have to wonder where the guy laughing with his teammates in this video has gone.

Something catches my eye. I stop the video and rewind it. A jarring hit one of the Penguins defensemen lays on him. A guy even bigger than Jake slams him into the wall. But what makes me gasp is not the crush of bodies when he's upright. It's when he hits the ice head first and gets knocked into the boards by the scrum of players fighting over the puck. His head caught in the middle of all that violence.

I watch him get to his feet a little wobbly, his bleeding face making it all the more gory. Then he skates off the ice. I watching that forty second clip three more times and make a mental note to ask him about it next time I see him.

That is, if I ever see him again.

My phone keeps chiming with notifications. Unlocking it, I stare at my screen. 5630 Twitter notifications. I've blocked so many accounts I've gotten them down to almost zero so this alarms me. It's possible someone took a screenshot of my tweet and circulated it again.

Reluctantly, I open Twitter and start to read. Then, I scream.

Chapter Thirteen

Music, bluesy with a hip hop edge, lures me into the bar. After bouncing around ideas for the next column with Hal and Gray, I decided to walk home instead of calling an Uber. I should be ecstatic. I should be celebrating. And yet I'm not. I'm pining…again.

My article was retweeted by a very famous daytime host whose name starts with the letter E. It has garnered thousands of likes. Twenty five thousand to be exact. That's a lot of eyeballs.

But back to the music. The Tri-Lakes has gone through a cultural revolution of sorts since I left for school, the music scene exploding, and most bars have one night a week they devote to showcasing local bands on the rise.

As big as the bar is, with its exposed red brick and industrial beams and pipes, it is packed. Both with locals and a large share of out-of-towners, the latter easily distinguishable by the designer clothes.

I cut through the press of bodies and head toward the

back, where the band is tuning their instruments getting ready to play another set.

By sheer luck, a group of girls at a table located against the wall is about to leave. One looks at me and asks if I want it. I don't, as a general rule, hang at bars by myself. But I can't bear to be alone tonight, and the music seems to be the antidote for whatever I'm feeling—which is sorry for myself.

So he left without saying goodbye or anything. Not even to tell me where he was going. I can't hold it against him. That wouldn't be fair. We have nothing but mutual attraction and a few scorching kisses between us.

Nodding, I take a seat and thank them as they leave. Layer after layer of clothing gets peeled off: Jackie's Ralph Lauren Navajo coat, my hat, gloves. We've had a snap of cold weather lately and even a few flurries. I don't care if it's May, I'm freezing, and it's safe to assume that I'll probably be freezing until sometime in August.

A waitress takes my order and quickly returns with my vodka cranberry. I rarely drink but this is one of those nights. All around me people are laughing and living their lives while I'm stuck in standby, waiting for something to break loose and set me free.

"To me," I mutter, raising the cocktail to my lips.

"And Ellen."

As the cosmo and music work their magic, soothing my weary soul, a prickle of awareness runs across the back of my neck. Without thought, I glance over my shoulder and catch sight of a familiar tall figure pushing through the crowd.

Head tipped back, eyes scanning the room. In his hand a beer bottle and the sleeve of thin black sweater pushed up his forearms. His dark blue gaze lands on me and he stops, staring for what feels like forever. Meanwhile my stomach does that funny thing it's not supposed to do whenever he looks at me.

"Hi," he says, reaching the table. He takes a seat.

"Hi," I say, confused by the swing of emotions I'm feeling—happy to see him and equally terrified that I'm feeling this way. "How was your trip?" God, did that come out snarky? Hopefully it's too loud in here for him to have noticed.

"Good…it was good." He looks away, over my shoulder, face tight with heavy thoughts. An awkward silence falls and I try to fill it, as I often do.

"Are you here for the music?"

His gaze returns to me, wanders over my face. The crease in between his brows disappears. "I was on my way to the paper and I saw you walk in."

"You did? I mean, you were?" I'm a bundle of nerves. Is he saying what I think he's saying?

"I went to see Karen—Mike's wife."

No, apparently he's not. Disappointment washes over me. He doesn't have to explain himself. We are nothing to each other. He owes me nothing.

"Is that…is that hard for you?" I take a big sip of my drink and feel it burn my throat.

He pauses, mulling over how to answer. "She's seeing someone and wanted to tell me in person."

He doesn't look okay with it. The sinking sensation in my gut stages a comeback. "I'm…I feel like I lose Mike more and more each day." His gaze drops, directed at the condensation on the beer bottle he's wiping away with his thumb. "Ask me. I know you want to."

It's been hanging there between us. Do I think people make honest mistakes? Yes. But this is bigger than that. So, heart pounding, I ask, "Were you drinking the night of the accident?"

Looking me squarely in the eyes, he says, "No."

"Drugs?"

"Not that night. I've used my fair share of painkillers, but that night I took over-the-counter."

The relief I feel is overwhelming.

"Are you mad at her for moving on?"

He shakes his head and exhales deeply. "No. No, I'm happy for her."

Now I'm the one exhaling deeply. I don't know what I would've done if he said yes. I'm past the point of denying that I don't have feelings for this man.

"I was coming to find you...I—"

A guy knocks into our table going backward, pushed by his buddy. Not a local. He's dressed top to bottom in designer clothes. The two-thousand-dollar Yeeze Nikes make my eyes roll.

"Sorry, yo," he says to us when he almost winds up in Jake's lap. Had Jake not grabbed the bottle fast enough, the beer would've spilled all over me.

Seeing Jake's expression, the dude laughs. He's high or drunk or both probably. "Easy, yo. It was an accident."

Then he flips his long bangs to the side. His friend steps up behind him and checks us out. And if guy number one is Dumb then this one is Dumber. Dumber has the oversized muscles of someone who feeds on a steady diet of steroids.

"I know this guy. You're Jake Turner. Amirite?" He

turns to his idiot friend who's standing way too close to our table for our comfort. "The hockey player. The one that killed the other guy—Bresler."

"Yo, I loved Bresler," Dumb says, expression stricken. "Damn, this is the guy that killed him?"

Listening to these two so cavalierly speak of Mike Bresler and Jake makes my blood boil. "Excuse me?" I say to both of them. "If you're done, can you move please."

"Whatever," one of then claps back.

"What did you say?"

"Don't," I hear in a soft rasp.

I glance sideways, mainly to assess Jake's mood—I've never known a man to have as many moods as this one does at any given moment—and find him totally chill. It's almost peculiar. "Why not?"

"Because you don't bring a squirt toy to a gun fight." He tips his chin at his arm resting on the table. My gaze follows his lead, and when it lands on his bicep, he flexes.

Oh please. I'm ready to flatten his overinflated ego with a well-deserved quip when I glance up. Only one small problem—I lose the power of speech. Whatever I was about to say drains out of my head because for the first time ever, Jake Turner, Scrooge of the Adirondacks, smiles. And it's not one of his evil little smirks. Or one of his teasing ones. It's the genuine article, the real deal. And the stunning part? This rare breed of smile reveals two perfectly matched dimples.

Somebody get the oxygen.

"Bresler was ten times the player you'll ever be, Turner." The guy's voice is louder this time around, his speech more slurred. I see this going badly.

"You're a loser, man!"

"Okay, that's it—" I can't contain myself anymore. I'm not prone to violence or temper tantrums, but listening to someone disparage him is doing strange things to me. A sense of protectiveness I never knew I was capable of pushes me to act, the feeling not a pleasant one or one I can ignore. "Punk ass kids…"

I get to my feet, the stool scraping loudly against the wood floor, and feel a big hand gently clasps my arm. We've had our ups and downs since meeting on that fateful night almost three months ago. I've gone from gratitude, to dislike, to physical attraction, to…to frankly really liking him. But this…this feels different. This feels bigger than all those other stages combined.

While I examine the strong tan fingers wrapped

around my arm, he tugs me closer. I'm close enough that I can see the scar across his top lip and three rogue freckles on his left cheekbone. Close enough that my heart starts racing as I watch his heavy-lidded gaze focus on my lips.

"Leave it be," he quietly tells me.

For a second, I get lost in the moment. The band hasn't started playing again and the volume in the bar has dialed down enough that it sounds like he and I are alone in the room.

"Someone needs to defend you if you aren't going to do it yourself."

His lashes lower as his eyes roam my face. "You wanna defend me, Carebear?"

"Somebody has to…and don't call me that." There's less than zero conviction in my voice, but I'm not ready to admit that I like it. That I like the way he says it. That I love the sound of my nickname in that deep, rough rasp.

It feels like defeat in a way. In fact, I sound embarrassingly breathy and I do not get breathy. And yet I do in the presence of an ex-hockey player with a penchant for frowns and primary colors.

"Yeah, listen to your bitch, Turner," declares the steroid abuser.

The smile drops and the dimples disappear. And the disappointment I feel at the loss of them is reason enough to give these two yahoos a beatdown.

Jake stands, and acting quickly, I lunge for his arm. Suddenly, I'm an accessory, dangling off of him. I'm 5'6" and he's 6'2" and he's literally wearing me.

"What did you say?" he murmurs at Dumb and Dumber.

"Turner, Turner! Leave it. Come on. I need to get home. How about you walk me? C'mon." He takes a step forward and the two idiots square up. Everyone else around us, finally taking notice of the kerfuffle, make room for the imminent barroom brawl. "I said leave it—this guy is a winter weather advisory."

That gets his attention. He stops and looks down at me, his lips quirking. "A what?"

"A winter weather advisory—one to three inches."

The dimples are back, his face slowly stretching into an ear to ear smile, white teeth showing and everything. One thing is clear, however. Smiling obviously does not come naturally to him because it looks like he doesn't know what to make of it.

"Come on…" he says to me a moment later, placing me back on my feet. "Let's get out of here."

Pulling a hundred-dollar bill out of the back pocket of his jeans, Turner stops one of the waitresses. He tells her to settle his tab and to keep the rest, her eyes lighting up when she sees the bill.

"Fucking chump," we hear one of the Dumb and Dumber twins say. Ignoring them, Jake wraps a steady arm around my shoulders and guides me toward the door.

I have to give credit where credit is due. I've always assumed hockey players were hotheads, lacking self-control and quick to pick a fight. Jake is no such thing. In fact, his self-control is something to admire.

"You're good at not letting the smack talk get to you…it's impressive."

He shrugs and holds the door open for me. "Decades of practice." Then he throws a sideways smirk and points to the bridge of his nose. "I wasn't always this good at it."

Outside things get very quiet and a little awkward, an elephant sitting between us. Jake starts walking in the direction of the Comfort Cottages and I hurry to keep up with his long strides. It's a cold clear night and a dusting of snow covers the ground from yesterdays freak snowfall.

"Why did you do that?" he says a few minutes later, puffs of cold air hanging by his mouth.

I take his wrist to stop him, and he turns to face me in front of a dark storefront lit by a Main Street lamppost. "Why do you let people talk to you like that?"

"What do you want me to say? They're right."

"Give me a break, Turner. It was an accident. It could've happened to anyone."

"Somebody died, Carrie." He starts walking again and I jog after him.

"So for the rest of your life you're going to take abuse from people? How long are you going to punish yourself?" I say a bit too loudly.

We pass a young couple headed in the opposite direction. They turn to stare before walking on toward the bars.

"Turner…Jesus Christ Superstar, slow down! I can't keep up with your oafishly long legs. Jake, c'mon!"

He slows enough for me to see he's hiding a smile.

"Hey, asshole. Miss us?" We both turn to find Dumb and Dumber standing ten feet away, all puffed out and looking for trouble. Crap.

In contrast, Jake's face is a portrait in serenity. Albeit with a slightly murdery undertone.

"Don't do it, Jake." I can see it now—a lawsuit, a possible arrest. His name in the news once again, which is his biggest nightmare. "Jake, please…" But he's not hearing me. He steps forward and I scuttle after him.

"You get one shot at this so make it a good one," he tells Dumber. "Then it's my turn."

Wearing matching sinister smiles, Dumb and Dumber glance at each other. Steroid Boy steps up and rolls his shoulders. Bouncing on his toes, he raises his fists while Jake stands perfectly still. Meanwhile, I fret in the background.

I mean, what do I do? Play accomplice to this mess? Get in the middle of it? I'm thinking if I get in the middle of this, I'll be the one knocked on my ass, and I will not be the dumb girl in this story.

Steroid Boy throws a punch and his fist connects with Jake's jaw. His head snaps to the side and I screech. It's violent and ugly and I immediately want to go check his face, but I take one step in his direction and he shakes his head at me.

Then it happens, lightening quick. Jake swings so fast at Steroid Boy that I don't realize what's happened until he's on the ground, squirming and moaning, holding his bleeding face while his friend laughs at him.

Carried Away

"C'mon, Carebear. Let's go home." He frowns at his knuckles and stretches his fingers. After which, Jake Turner, painter, fighter, one-time hockey God, takes me by the hand and leads me there.

* * *

"Of all the idiotic things…" I soak a cotton ball with hydrogen peroxide and step closer. "You could've been sued."

As soon as we got back to the cottages, I dragged him—under heavy protest—into the Austen and ordered him to sit on the pink tufted armchair. The punch split his lip open and his jaw is swollen. He needs medical attention even if he did chuckle sarcastically when I told him so.

Seeing him now all big and dark perched on a delicate pink chair brings a halfcocked grin to my face.

"What are you smiling at?"

I'm standing and yet we're almost face to face. "You. In that chair."

"You still think you have to live in a big city to have a grand adventure?"

I chew on that for a moment. Since I landed in Albany, everyday has been an adventure. "I think I've had my fill of adventures for a while. Bailing you out of jail would've been my limit for the year."

"You weren't worried he'd hurt me?" he says in a mocking tone. Stepping between his splayed knees, I grab a chunk of his hair and push his head back, dabbing the cotton on the corner of his bottom lip. He winces when the peroxide hits the cut.

"Maybe I should've. If a little sting gets a reaction, you're not the D-man I thought you were."

His lips fight the smile wanting to grow, but he loses that fight. When he does, the dimples make another appearance, and I find myself smiling along with him.

"Who do you think I am now?"

It's the inflection in his deep voice that makes me raise my eyes to his, the cotton ball suspended in mid-air. Something in that question tells me the answer is important to him. Or maybe I'm imagining it. Regardless, I can't be flip about it. I can't be anything other than completely honest. This moment feels too important.

"I think you're more sensitive than you want people to know. I think that you have a fragile heart and that you protect it fiercely...I think that I want a tenth of your self-control."

Done with the cleaning of the cut, I toss the cotton ball down on the table with the rest of the first-aid materials.

"I think you're an incredibly talented artist…and I think you must have veneers because no one with a career as long as yours could still have all his teeth."

Raising his index finger, he points to an incisor and the tooth next to it. "This one and this one. But that's it."

The moment expands, changes into something else. This isn't our usual back and forth dance. This is something meaningful. Despite that he's not at all what I would pick for myself, despite that I'm leaving and he's staying, despite that he's barely civil most of the time, I think I'm falling for him.

Jake is unexpectedly thoughtful and kind. He's selfless and honest. And part of me feels ashamed that I stepped in it once again, assuming the worst about him based on what I learned from the press.

His thighs close gently around my legs, and he leans forward. My body comes alive with the knowledge that I'm about to be kissed. Even better, I'm about to be kissed by a man *I* want to kiss. My skin feels sunburnt under my long sleeve shirt and a suspicious heat grows between my legs. And all I have to say is thank God I have my good underwear on.

His soft lips press against mine and I breathe out a

sigh of relief.

This...this is a kiss. That's the thing with a really great kiss—you can't explain the feeling, but you know it when you feel it.

A current of awareness runs over my skin and up my back as he ever so gently savages my mouth. Slowly, he rises from the chair, pulling me in, curving his big body around mine. His hands are in my hair, holding my head like it's a sacred treasure.

There's no time to think, there's no need. I am gone. Wrapped up in him, consumed by the need to get closer. And I do. I want to get closer so badly I can hardly stand it.

My hands grip and knead his arms. Too wide for me to get my fingers around, they travel over his shoulders and down his broad chest covered in fine wool, and he sighs, sighs! sweet heaven's sake.

"Jake...Jake...Jake..." I hear my voice echo. It sounds like a faraway supplication, my tongue and lips shaping the words in between tender teasing kisses.

He pulls away and searches my face, amusement dancing in his indigo eyes. "What?" he whispers, punctuating it with another kiss.

"Nothing," I murmur back, so ridiculously happy I'm

floating, giddy with the anticipation of more. "I just like the feel of your name of my lips."

His smile slowly fades as he stares at me. And when he kisses me again, he does it softly, reverently, like he's planning on making it last forever. Like this is all there is and the only place he wants to be. For the first time since we've met, Jake Turner is living in the moment, and that moment is me.

"*I'm going back to Cali, Cali, Cali. I'm going back to Cali…*" my phone rings, the tone courtesy of LL Cool J. "*I'm going back to Cali…*"

Jake pulls away and we both stare at my phone sitting on the tabletop, Ben's name flashing on the screen. It's a total mood killer and Jake's expression proves it.

"You should get that," he says over the sound on the music.

But I don't want to get it. I want to get back to kissing and possibly more. "Jake."

Walking backwards, he reaches the front door of the cottage. "Jake wait…" Damnit, I want to cry. It's been years! And the last time wasn't exactly all that memorable.

"You should get that."

Rooted to the floor, I stand in the middle of the

cottage, completely powerless as I watch all the amazing feelings flowing between us a minute ago disappear without a trace like they never even happened.

Jake walks out and the phone continues to ring. Instead of leaving a message the traitorous rat hung up and redialed.

"Yes?" I answer, my tone making it clear that I'm less than happy to hear from him.

"Carrie. Fucking Christ, I've been trying to get a hold of you for a week. You have to come back. Kennedy is a mess. She can't do anything without me having to hold her hand. Legal is up my arse because she didn't follow up on a source and half my dry cleaning is missing."

Ben sounds frazzled. Ben is never frazzled. I am secretly pleased at this new development in his character. But this is no longer about Ben. It's about me and a fork in the road, so to speak.

"Ben…"

"Yes?"

"I'm sorry about Kennedy."

"Great. So when can I expect you? By the way, where are you? I went by your place and the old lady next door, the one with the cat, told me you'd moved."

"Lake Placid…New York"—by eyes drift to the wall I

share with Jake—"and I'm not coming back yet. But I do have a suggestion."

"I need you, I don't need suggestions."

Yeah, he needs his slave back. No thanks. It dawns upon me then. Falls out of thin air and hits me in the head. Getting fired may have been the best thing to ever happen to me.

I stare at the wall that separates my cottage from Jake's. The second best.

"Ben…"

"Yes?"

There are moments in life when one must practice restraint. This is not one of those moments.

"Go fuck yourself."

Chapter Fourteen

REGINA AND I HEAD TO the Farmer's Market the following day. I need inspiration for my next article. The first person we run into is Beth Herman, one of the mean girls that used to terrorize us at lunch. In tow, she has four-year-old twin girls and one tired looking husband.

"Gina Polizzi and Carrie Anderson! Oh my Gawd. It's so good to see you two. And you're still friends. How cute!"

The feeling is not mutual. To my regret, she looks exactly the same. Small, blonde, and beautiful.

We make polite conversation, and she tells me how much she loved the article. "Brad and I are donating. Those poor poor boys. It's terrible. And it's so great that that hockey player"—she turns to her husband—"Honey, what's his name?"

"Turner. Jake Turner."

"Yeah, that's right. It's so nice that he does the lessons." She cups her hand near her mouth. "Madison says he's smoking hot. She's got it bad for him."

Madison can go pound salt.

She turns again. "Honey, one minute." Honey looks like he wants to swallow a gun.

She takes us aside, out of earshot of her family, and what comes next surprises everyone.

Beth starts crying.

She goes on and on about how many times she thought of all the awful things she'd said to us over the years. She says that now that she has kids she can't imagine someone, anyone, treating her girls that way. Honestly, I wish she would've had her *come to Jesus* moment a little sooner. Like a decade sooner. But I accept the apology now nonetheless. After the Sean Gorman incident, this is a big deal.

It's twilight by the time I get back to the Cottages. I smile the entire walk home, a sense of satisfaction reaching deep into my bones that I haven't felt since breaking my big story all those years ago. Things are definitely looking up for me.

On my way back to the Austen, I think about Jake and wonder what he's up to. I even contemplate knocking on his door. Except, I never know which Jake I'm going to get. I have no idea how Mr. Unpredictable will behave. And since I'm not ready to come down from the high of today's victory, I scrap the plan.

As I'm passing by the house, I spot a tall figure under the porch light. He looks like my father, but it couldn't be him. It couldn't because this man is standing awfully close to a woman with shoulder length brown hair, their posture undeniably intimate. And everyone knows my father doesn't date.

Until I draw closer and I see the smile. Holy crap, it is my father. This is major breaking news. Great news, in fact.

Pulling my phone out of my tote, I text my sister.

Me: Alert. Alert. Eugene Anderson is finally romancing a woman!! Hallelujah and praise the Lawd.

An incoming text rings, and I immediately mute it. My father and the mystery woman are talking in whispery words, and I don't want to be caught perving on them.

Jackattack: OMG!!!!!!

Meanwhile, just like a perv, exactly like a perv, I creep closer and crouch behind an azalea bush. Which is when my sister calls.

"I can't talk and spy at the same time!" I whisper hiss.

"What does she look like?" Jackie whispers back.

"Did you not hear me? Hold on—" I glance at them again. "Tall, thin, brown hair. Dressed kinda shabby in worn jeans and a chunky, faded blue sweater."

"Eh, I dunno," my sister, the bitch, says. "Dad deserves better than that."

"What are you talking about?! That's exactly what Dad needs. I'll tell you what he *doesn't* need—another social climber that will ask him to make changes he's not ready to make. Like sell the hotel and travel the world. Dad would hate that."

My sister laughs. "Who are you, Dr, Phil now? Don't draw up the marriage contract yet. She might be a vendor."

"Yeah? You stroke your vendor's hair when he makes a delivery to the office?"

"Never mind," she says, giggling.

For years we've been gently trying to encourage him to date. My father has the biggest heart and so much life to live. He should share it with someone that values and worships him. He doesn't deserve to be alone for the rest of his life because he was burned by one conniving fraudster.

"Oh, oh, Jackie I gotta go. I think he's going to kiss her and I need to get closer!"

"Don't hang up on me! Wait! Take pictures—" I hear Jackie hiss right before I hang up. Take pictures...the hormones are making her crazy.

Sticking my phone in the back pocket of my black skinny jeans, I move from the azalea bush to the evergreen hedge.

They're standing even closer now, huddled together. I watch as he leans down and places a brief kiss on her lips, this mystery woman who seems to have stolen his heart right from underneath my nose. She must have because knowing my Dad, he wouldn't be here with her if he didn't have feelings.

It's about bloody time.

He's wasted too many of good years pining for Zelda. I know more than a few single women in town who have been going after him with a full court press only to be disappointed with a gentle rebuttal.

"What are you doing?" a scratchy male voice inquires.

Startled, I whip around. Jake is standing halfway between my cottage and the hedge, approximately ten feet away from me. The volume of his voice is way too high for lurking and spying so I make a face and place my index finger over my mouth. That's when I notice his attire. Or lack thereof. He's shirtless and sweaty, taking deep breaths from the run he just returned from.

Without a word, he marches over, his black silky shorts clinging to every muscle as he walks. Other parts too, but I do my best not to stare. I mean, I'm not a total savage. His chest, however, is fair game. Needless to say, I look my fill.

"What are you doing?" he repeats in a completely regular volume.

"Nothing. Nothing. I'm doing nothing. Shhhh."

Popping out his ear pods, he studies me, then follows my line of sight. "That's strange because it looks like you're spying on your father."

"Keep your voice down!" I whisper. "And bend your knees. Get down or he'll see you."

Crouching next to me, he places his hands on his knees and watches me while I watch my dad. "This is wrong."

"Duly noted. Now can you please shhhhush."

He's so close his bare arm brushes up against mine and my pulse quickens. Although I have a sweater on, it doesn't change the fact that I can feel him. It's a narcotic to the senses—and completely distracting. There should be a warning label taped to his ass.

"Stop staring at me," I mutter.

"Why? You don't like it?"

My lips quiver with the need to laugh. Funny Jake might be my favorite Jake. "No. It's distracting. You're distracting me while I'm in the middle of some very important investigative work."

"You're spying on your dad."

"Whatever," I hiss, and bite down on my lip to school the grin. It'll only encourage him to continue.

Meanwhile, across the way, the heat between the mystery lady and my dad turns up to medium hot. And while I watch, I'm increasingly reminded that it was only a few days ago that Jake and I were doing much of the same and worse.

He hasn't broached the subject and neither will I. It's not like I can just *ask* him what he's thinking. For instance, if he liked it as much as I did. If he still thinks we have chemistry. For all I know, he's had his taste and has lost interest. The latter may actually break me.

The kiss turns passionate, and a growing feeling of discomfort crawls over my skin. Jake's right. This is wrong. Maybe spying, surveilling, whatever isn't such a hot idea. I'm about to walk away when they pull apart, and Dad opens the back door to the family residence.

Oh my God, he's having this woman sleep over for the night!

I'm seconds from calling Jackie and dropping this bombshell in her lap when another one explodes right in my face.

The mystery woman turns and the ground beneath my feet evaporates.

It's Zelda.

All the blood leaves my face. I blink and blink, trying to make her disappear but it doesn't happen. It doesn't stop me from trying again, however. Vaguely, I can feel Jake's strong, stoic presence next to me, but everything else is white noise at this point.

Automatically, I stand, back rod-straight. Whether they see me or not is no longer a factor because I march across the lawn after them.

"Carrie," I hear tailing me.

Horrified, bewildered, disgusted, I watch my father, the man I've always counted on to give me the unvarnished truth, grin at the woman who abandoned us. Without thought, I make a beeline for them. I don't know why, but I'm not really thinking right now. I'm pissed and I want answers.

"What are you doing here?" I snap when I reach the

bottom of the porch stairs.

Startled, they spin around to face me. Dad blanches, his face going from surprise to guilt. But Zelda? She's as nonchalant as ever. Not a care in the world. So typical.

She smiles softly. "Carrie, hi sweetie—"

"Save your pet names."

"I've been trying to reach you."

"Yeah, I know," I tell her. "That's why I don't answer my phone. Why is that hard for you to understand?"

I can't be nice right now. I'm much too angry to be rational. Besides, when someone doesn't call you back, isn't it obvious that you've been canceled?

"Dad?" My accusing glare shifts between the two of them. My father looks like a kid caught with his hand in the human cookie jar.

He runs a hand through his gray hair and sighs. "What do you want me to say, Carrie?"

"I want you to remember that this woman left us."

Dad winces and Zelda frowns. "Gene, don't let her speak to you like that."

"Why are you even here? Haven't you wreaked enough destruction in his life? I mean, I know destroying people is your bloodsport but can't you find someone else to torture?"

"Carrie…" Jake takes me by the bicep and I shake him off.

"No."

Zelda steps forward and I take note of the changes. The muted hair, the absence of heavy makeup and Botox. The clothes…for shit's sake the clothes are laughable. It's like she's trying to play the part of dutiful country wife.

"I know this is going to be hard for you to hear, but I still care very much about your father…" Pausing, she glances back at Dad. "I never stopped loving him."

I'm about to lose my mind. For once, Zelda looks unsure, and it emboldens me. "You have got to be fucking kidding me!"

"Carrie! You know I hate that language," Dad, the bastion of moral rectitude chimes in. The one who has been sneaking round for who knows how long.

"How long have you been seeing her?" Silence. A sneaking suspicion worms its way in. "You've been seeing each other for weeks, haven't you? Maybe months. I'm pretty sure I saw you at the grocery store."

No one says a word. But there's plenty of awkward to pass around.

I glance over my shoulder, at Jake, whose expression turns somewhat sheepish. He scratches the back of his neck and breaks eye contact. "That's why you picked me up that night at Regina's bar. Don't bother answering."

I turn my ire back on my mother. "Remember when you were a lesbian?"

"Bisexual, honey. And I still am."

"Dad!"

"You can't help who you love, Carrie," my father says, trying to justify Zelda's betrayal while looking frustrated and upset. That's no easy task and yet he manages it. I cannot believe how cavalier he's being about this. About a woman who cheated on him repeatedly.

"Even if that person occasionally loves other women!" My face is on fire, my buns coming undone.

"I never loved Joan," Zelda replies, inserting herself again. "But I did care for her. And will forever be grateful that she assisted in my self-actualization—"

"Gahhh! That's even worse! You're a sociopath," I scream at the night sky. "I...I can't with this steaming pile of garbage right now!"

Turning, I walk away, heading for the quiet refuge of the Austen. That woman's mind was a treasure. She had the foresight to know we would all need to escape reality from time to time.

Carried Away

I'm about to take the porch steps two at a time when I pivot and head for the lake instead. I need to feel something other than burning rage.

Although it's almost the end of May, it's far from warm. In fact, I'm still wearing a winter jacket most of the time. The only one immune to the cold seems to be Jake.

Doesn't matter. I'm red hot mad and no amount of cold can touch this. I reach the edge of the lake and don't stop, some invisible force drawing me in. Kicking off my Golden Goose sneakers without breaking stride, I walk straight into the frigid lake.

"Carrie!" The sound reaches me and drowns as I dunk my head under water, my entire body convulsing from the near freezing temperature. The oxygen in my lungs turns solid. That's what it feels like. I feel turned to stone.

A strong hand grips my arm and yanks me up, the motion jarring and painful. I break the surface and take a deep gasping breath. Under oath, I would swear both my lungs collapsed. That's how painful it is to breathe.

Jake drags me out of the water none too gently. The weight of my clothes soaked straight through makes it impossible to take a single step. It's like walking in quicksand. Seeing that he's practically naked, he doesn't have this problem.

Tired beyond measure, I collapse on the sand of the shoreline coughing and spitting up water while he stands over me with his hands on his hips. Looking up, I'm faced with his cold anger, his chest rising and falling rapidly with each labored breath he takes.

"Well that was fucking stupid. We need to get you inside before you go hypothermic."

He offers me his hand and I offer mine back. He mutters something and squats, hooks his arms under my pits and lifts me. As soon as he does, I wrap my arms and legs around him, holding on for dear life. Seems like I've been doing a lot of that with Jake lately.

Teeth chattering, I bury my face in the slope of his shoulder and dig in, desperate to get warm. I'm so cold my lips are turning numb. Every attempt to speaks produces nothing other than gibberish.

"Don't talk….we can talk later." He pats my back and begins climbing the hill back up to the cottages.

An eternity passes before we cross the threshold of his cottage and head for the bathroom. He carries me inside and sets me on my feet. Then he turns on the shower at full blast.

"Jake…"

"Just…wait."

Hot steam fills the room in minutes. It gets into my lungs and thaws them, soothes the burning pain. My body shaking violently, I lean on Jake. It's become common practice anyway. His is the only solid, steady strength I can count on these days. Which probably doesn't bode well for me in the long run. I tuck the thought away to examine later.

When the shower hits the right temperature, he takes my arm and drags me inside the shower with him. Three years ago my father upgraded all the bathrooms to have large standing showers with massage shower heads and wall jets. Thank God for small favors. Otherwise both of us couldn't have fit in it now.

Jake sinks to the floor and I follow. He wraps his arms around me, and I lean back against his chest, cradled between his legs. Then he holds me until I stop shaking. Until the cold in my bones and in my heart gives way to other feelings.

"Hey, hey, don't cry. C'mon, babe."

Babe?

"…I didn't mean to yell at you…you know I don't mean it…" he murmurs in my ear, sneaking a kiss in here and there that makes me shiver for all the right reason. "I mean…it was stupid—running into the water like that. Don't get me wrong. What I mean is…"

He really cannot handle feminine tears. I should tell him that I cry when I'm angry…and sad…and happy. But maybe I'll let him hold me a little longer before I do.

* * *

"Get in," he says, standing before me in a pair of black boxer briefs.

His body is a stunning work of art, a perfect balance of muscle and bone, now that I get to see it in its full glory. Too bad I'm so tired I can barely keep my eyes open to truly enjoy it.

After Jake washed my hair and rinsed it, he left the bathroom to fetch me a pair of his boxers and a t-shirt while I peeled the wet clothes off. If he's not careful, there's a very good chance I may fall in love with him.

"I'm sleeping here?" I ask, more than a little timidly because God forbid I misunderstood. I'm so twisted and tired I'm capable of all sorts of screw-ups right now.

"You shouldn't be alone."

That seems to end the debate. I slide beneath his cool sheets, and he goes to the kitchen to fetch me a bottle of water.

He turns the lamp off, and the room is plunged in darkness with only a dim light coming through the window. He slips into bed next to me, and without hesitation wraps me in his arms, pulling me against him. It's all I can do not to sigh.

"Thank you for rescuing me again. That's all you seem to be doing lately." Shame makes my cheeks hot.

"Stop apologizing." He takes my hand and places it on his chest. His skin is burning hot under my palm, the fine hair on his chest soft.

"What was all that about? She's your mother, Carrie."

"My mother left us when I was ten."

"Whatever she did to Gene, it's their business."

The anger boils up again. "The summer I turned nine she got into the habit of taking me to see a movie a few times a week. I wasn't in summer camp yet and Jackie was, so she couldn't babysit. I thought it was great. I got to sit in a dark theater and eat candy. Soon enough we ran out of movies locally, so we had to travel farther and farther to larger movie theaters. She would leave me there and come to pick me up at the end.

"One day I ate too much candy and started throwing up. The kid working there rushed to help me and when he realized I was there alone he called the cops. That's how my father found out my mother was having an affair."

"Jesus. It's bad. I get it but…"

"But what?"

"But at least you have one."

I didn't think I could feel any worse tonight but here we are. "I'm sorry…how did she die?"

"Heart attack. Bad valve. It failed when she was at work at the diner. She was a waitress. We didn't have any money for doctors so she never knew."

"How did you find out?"

"She worked the night shift. There was a knock on our door one night around midnight. The cops found me home alone and called CPS."

"And your dad?"

I hear him take a deep breath. "I met him once—when I was six. But all I remember about him is that he was big and scary. To a six year old he was scary. I think…I got the impression we were better off without him."

My throat swells and my eyes get glassy. I take a shaky breath and reach for him, cupping his scratchy jaw. Guided by nothing but touch. It's automatic and without design. He kisses my palm brings my hand down. Then he turns me and tucks me against the front of his body.

"Sleep," he mutters tiredly. "We both need it."

Chapter Fifteen

"Heard you had quite the tussle last night," Nan says the moment I step into the kitchen the next morning.

For a moment I think she means Jake and then I remember.

"Did you hear about the hooker?" I ask while I pour fresh coffee grinds in the machine.

"She's you mother. Watch your mouth," she says, pointing two manicured fingers at me with an unlit cigarette between them. An eye roll worthy moment if ever there was one. "And yes."

I turn on my heels to get a good look at my grandmother. Something doesn't smell right, and my suspicion is confirmed when I see the blank look on her face.

"You knew. You knew and you didn't tell me."

"Not my business to tell." She grabs a mug from the cabinet and pours herself a cup of coffee. Then she lights the cigarette.

"Nan…" I hate the smell.

"My house, my rules."

"And you're okay with this? Your son cavorting with a woman of loose morals?"

"Morning," my father says stepping into the kitchen.

"Morning…" I mutter.

"We were just talking about you," Nan announces.

Dad exhales tiredly. "Let's have it out. But once it's done, I will not discuss it anymore."

"Dad…how can you possibly trust her? She's an energy vampire. She will drain you until there's nothing left and toss you aside."

"Carrie…" He makes a pained face. "I don't expect you to understand."

"I don't."

He sighs tiredly and meets my pointed gaze. "We don't get to pick the people we love."

There's a lot of truth to that. But it's the look on his face that practically knocks me off my feet. He means it.

"I can't explain it any other way," he starts again. "I have always loved your mother. And it's a sure bet I always will."

* * *

"I can't believe these numbers." Hal looks dazed as he stares at his computer screen. We moved our weekly meeting to late afternoon so it wouldn't interfere with my work at the hotel.

My column has gone viral. Twitter has even given me a blue check. That means a lot in some circles. Not so much in others.

"You know what this means…" Gray says, his big brown eyes full of mischief and mayhem. "Syndication."

"Slow your roll, Edward R. Murrow. A few more eyeballs don't equate to squat."

I've been having so much fun writing my lifestyle columns that I forgot to worry about everything else. Like Shares and Likes and reTweets. I stopped paying attention and it happened. And nobody is more surprised than I am.

Every time I walk into the office, Hal is hollering about the sky-rocketing numbers like he hit the trifecta at Saratoga. I guess small town life is more entertaining than I thought. Then again, I tend to be wrong a lot.

"This is cause for a celebration. Want to grab a drink?" Gray suggests.

"Yeah, I know just the place. Hal?"

He shakes his head.

My mind immediately drifts to Jake and our late night talk. I can either continue to live on standby, or I can go for it. And since I don't have his number, I figure one drink to shore up my spotty confidence, and then I knock on his door.

* * *

"What are you doing here?" Regina says to Gray the moment we reach the bar.

Her attention shifts back and forth between the two of us. "You two know each other?"

It's so loud in here I can barely hear her, the bar packed three rows deep.

"G—we work together at The Gazette. How do *you* two know each other?"

Gina's face goes blank. "He rents my guest house," she screams back.

"Hey," Gray says to my friend.

"Hello," Gina answers more coldly than I've ever seen her.

Well this is interesting. If I didn't know better, I'd say there are some serious vibes of the sexual variety swirling around here. Except I know better, and Gina likes them older—a lot older. Last guy she dated was forty-five.

We order and since it's a Thursday night there's no chance in hell we're getting a table. I'm slowly sipping my drink when someone bumps into me from behind. The guy apologizes and offers to buy me a drink. I show him I already have one and he moves on.

"I'll be right back," Gray yells in my ear. I nod and watch him take off, pushing through the crowd.

A few minutes later I'm standing alone when the guy who bumped into me earlier swings back around. "Hey, good timing, he says pointing to my empty glass. "Can I get you another?"

"No, dude. She's with me."

My attention jerks up…to find Jake standing behind the guy. He's dressed in black and looking like the return of the Grim Reaper, his face arranged in a harsh expression. And yet my stomach flips and my heart flutters. This is baaaad.

"Hi."

"Let's get out of here," he says to me.

Just like that. Like he expects me to obey. "I'm with friends."

"Yeah, she's with me," the guy who wants to buy me a drink says. It actually surprises me to see him still standing there.

"I'm not with him," I say to Jake. Then turn to glare at the guy. "I don't even know you." My eyes skip right back to Jake. "I'm with Gray."

"Who's Gray?" both Jake and the guy say.

"I'm Gray," Gray says, suddenly appearing behind me.

"Let's go," Jake says. And now I'm on the way to getting a little angry. He leaves town without a word, but I have to jump through hoops like a trained seal the minute he snaps his fingers?

"No."

"Carrie…"

"I'm here with friends, Jake. Stay or go, but I'm staying."

"Man, you're gonna let your girl talk to you like that?" the drink guy says.

"Shut up," both Jake and I answer.

He stares at me for a beat, then his glare moves to Gray. Then he turns and walks out.

* * *

Two hours later I'm back at the Austen.

"Did you have fun with what's-his-name?"

The question comes from the man sitting in the dark on the porch of his cottage, lawn chair tipped back and legs resting on the railing.

Oh, the drama.

I sat in a corner pounding Diet Cokes by myself because there was no way I was coming back here to give him the satisfaction. I'm not putting up with that nonsense from someone I have no claim on.

"Yes, I did. Thanks for asking. And his name is Gray." He cannot be seriously jealous of Gray. This cannot be why he's acting a fool. "Did you enjoy making an ass out of yourself?"

He takes a pull of his beer and sits upright, his chair thumping on the hollow wood.

"No, I didn't."

"Gray works with me at the paper. He's a friend, and you were rude to him. Look around you, Jake. I don't exactly have a ton of those so I would like to keep him."

"I'm your friend," he says quietly.

"Are you? Because you sure don't act like it sometimes. One minute you're hot. The next you're cold. I can't keep up with you anymore. You have more moods than I did when I was thirteen!"

"Shut up!" someone in the Whitman cottage shouts.

I slap my hands over my mouth muffling a burst of laughter. "Inside," I whisper, pointing to the Austen.

Without a backward glance, I walk into the cottage, unsure if he'll follow, but a minute later he shuts the door behind him. His head hung low, his hands shoved in the pockets of his jeans, every inch of him looking as remorseful as he should.

"I didn't mean to embarrass you," he says to the carpet. "I'm sorry." His gaze lifts to mine and the heat I find there is unmistakable. "I wanted you to myself tonight and I didn't handle it well."

Somebody beat on my chest. I think I just flatlined. Remorseful Jake is my favorite Jake so far, so sexy I want to peel that black t-shirt off his body with my teeth. Or maybe I'll just let him take mine off first.

He steps closer and a thought hits me. "Jake, I'm leaving."

His brows lower. "You're leaving?"

"Not now…not tomorrow. But someday soon. I'm going back to L.A. the first chance I get."

He looks away, thoughtful. "If this is your way of telling me you don't want this, just say so."

Turning, he walks out before I've gotten a chance to sort out all the strange and wonderful ways his mind works. I mean, sensitive is an understatement.

Snapping out of it, I chase after him, rip the door open, and jump out onto the porch.

"Wait…wait…wait!" I say to the broad back at the

bottom of my stairs.

He stops and turns slowly, looking thoroughly harassed, frustrated, and ready to walk away never to return again.

"What?" he huffs. And I beat back the urge to smile. My goodness, I'm crazy about this man and all of his million moods.

"Don't go."

His expression softens—marginally. No one else would notice the change, but I've gotten pretty good at reading all the subtle nuances of his beautiful face.

"Don't go, Jake," I say, stepping closer. I place one foot in front of the other down the front steps of the Austen, closing the distance between us while his dark blue eyes bore into mine, anticipation and doubt warring there.

"Give me a reason to stay," he replies, his scratchy voice holding a challenge.

A smile threatens to break out across my face because I can see his want and need getting the better of him.

Gathering every ounce of hard-fought courage I possess, I push the words out of my mouth. "Come back inside and I'll give you more than one."

When I reach the second to last step, we're eye to eye.

It's then I see it cross his face. The insecurity just beneath the surface of all that tough shell.

"Tell me you want me first," he murmurs, searching for signs of doubt on my face that he will not find.

All in, I wrap my arms around his neck and he pulls me closer. His breathing deepens, his chest pushing against my breasts.

"I want you. I want you desperately," I say against his lips. The scent of his soap and shampoo fill my lungs and it's like coming home. The way he feels in my arms, the way he smells, the sound of his voice. We've known each other only four months, but it feels like the span of a lifetime.

"Get a goddamn room!" Another shout from the Whitman cottage.

Jake kisses me. I wrap my legs around his waist and he carries me inside. And we don't stop kissing. We don't stop when he pushes me up against the wall and pins his hips hard against mine—almost painfully hard. But it only makes me want him more. And we don't stop when the pantings are knocked off the wall.

"I can't…I can't wait another minute," he mutters into my mouth. His tongue sliding against mine.

Clutching at the back of his shirt, I start to clumsily

yank it over his head. I need to feel him. I need to feel every inch of skin on his body. Last night was the biggest tease. If I hadn't been completely wrecked by the circumstances, I would not have slept a single minute. It was certainly bad enough when I awoke at 4 a.m. with his erection pressed up against my butt. He went for a run and I spent the next hour fantasizing about him.

Pulling away he places me on my feet and reaches for my blouse. Then he stops and meets my eyes.

"I need you."

The declaration is so heartfelt I feel the weight of it pressing down on me.

I push his hands down and grab the bottom of his shirt, pull it off of him.

"I need you too."

I run my hands up and down his chest and watch him take sharp, shallow breaths. My shirt comes off next. Then his jeans. Then mine. He picks me up and carries me to the bed, laying me down gently.

"I meant it when I told you I haven't been with anyone in three years."

It takes me back to the scene at the supermarket. Seems like a lifetime ago.

"I didn't mean any of the rest. You're beautiful,

Carrie. So fucking beautiful…" He swallows. His gaze moves away and comes right back to me. "The truth is I wanted you back then, but I didn't think I deserved someone like you."

Kill me know. Take the poison and plunge it straight into my veins because the sweet look on his face is too painful to bear.

I'm reminded of everything I said about him and shame turns me red hot.

"Jake, I didn't mean it either. Not a word. You know that, right?" He kisses me again, and this time I pull back. "And I haven't been with anyone even longer than that."

He gets up from the bed and pushes his boxer briefs down his well-muscled legs. His erection springs free, more than ready to get the job done.

"I'm on the pill," I tell him. "For my skin."

Slowly climbing on the bed, he reaches for my bra and I help him remove it. My panties next. His hand slips between my legs and enters me while his mouth latches onto my breast.

He hits all my sweet spots, and for the first time in my life, I get a real glimpse at what Jackie meant when she said she just knew.

Pushing my knees apart, he gets on top and anchors me to the bed, grinding against me until I'm a hair's breadth from coming.

"Jake…" I beg. He flexes his hips, entering me in one fluid motion. Big, hard, and ready. Stiffening, I hold my breath.

At first, it hurts. I haven't had sex in so long I almost don't remember it.

"I'll make it good for you. I promise…just hold onto me," he whispers and and starts gently rocking against me.

That's all it takes for my body to accept his. For me to let go and let him take over. Jake makes love like he does everything else, with patience and skill and total devotion. Piece by piece he takes me apart and puts me back together, leaving not a single part of me uncharted.

It's all I can do not to die of pleasure because the voice in the back of my head tells me this is special and unique. That it's something to be valued.

I come hard and long, with him deep inside of me. He follows after a few more thrusts. It's perfect. It's everything I hoped it would be. And as I'm falling asleep I think to myself, "Don't go away."

He squeezes me tighter and I hear him whisper, "Not

a chance."

Chapter Sixteen

Sex. Sex. And more sex. I have sex in the morning. I have it at night. I have it in the shower. Against the wall—not my favorite. On the kitchen table. On the floor. I still have the rug burns to prove it. It's safe to say Jake and I are sexually compatible.

No bad sushi in sight.

So naturally, when my dirty pirate of a sister calls, I assume she wants to discuss sex.

Jackie's face appears on my phone. I hit reject and think nothing of it. It's late at night. Jake is sound asleep next to me and I'm in the middle of writing.

Fact: you never want to interrupt the muse when she's whispering in your ear.

Except Jackie calls back. My sister can be a little demanding so I rinse and repeat, pushing her to voicemail.

The third time she calls, however, I answer without hesitation. Two calls means Jackie wants to rant. Three means there's a legit issue and it's not about the pair of

Manolos she saw on sale.

"Hey, what's up," I answer, tiptoeing out of bed and into the bathroom.

The nervous fluttering in my belly kicks into overdrive when I hear a sniffle. "Jackie?? What is it? Are you okay?"

"Yes." Voice broken, she takes a shaky breath. Whatever has gotten her this upset is nearly palpable. She's clearly crying, but I try not to assume the worst just yet. I don't want to speculate about my sister losing this baby because then I would have to speculate about how I'm going to glue her back together.

"What's wrong?"

"I need to tell you something."

Cryptic is not my sister's thing. Despite being a high powered corporate attorney, Jackie is a total straight shooter. "You can talk to me, but are you alright? Do I need to call an ambulance? Where's Charlie?"

"Charlie's at Sam's." She sighs tiredly. "We had a fight."

Sam is Charlie's brother so that sounds kosher, but Charlie and Jackie never fight. Like ever. I cannot remember a single fight they have ever had. They have *discussions*. Not fights.

"You want to tell me about it?" I gently prod. She's fragile right now. The last thing she needs is someone bearing down on her.

"I'm spotting again."

My stomach sinks. "What did the doctor say? Did you call him?"

"He says it's fine. Everything looks fine. The baby is fine. Charlie thinks everything's fine…everybody keeps telling me it's fine! I'm the only one that's not fine." Her soft cry filters through the phone and claws at my heart. Tears well in my eyes. "I'm not fine at all."

"If the doctor—"

"I think I'm being punished," she whispers, cutting me off.

She's not making any sense now. "Why would you think that? You're just under a lot of stress right now, but if the doctor thinks you're not in any danger of losing the baby…"

"I had an abortion, Carrie."

There's an acute pain in my chest. Like my heart was sucker punched right out. "Jackie, you're worrying me. Let me Call Charlie—"

"When I was in high school," she rushes to explain. I breathe an enormous sigh of relief. She's got a month left until her due date and that day can't come soon enough. "I was seventeen, and, and I...I...I just couldn't be pregnant. I couldn't do it. I was heading to Stanford that fall and I had my entire life ahead of me...I couldn't have a baby with *James* of all people. Do you remember him?"

My head is spinning with everything she's throwing at me. It's hard to keep up at this point. I was in junior high when Jackie was a senior so I vaguely recall the guy she was dating that year.

Regardless, it sounds like she's been stewing about this for some time so I decide it's best for her to vent, to let her get it all off her chest.

"A little. Does Dad know?"

"No...Nan does. She took me."

That knocks the wind out of me. I'm too stunned to speak, and in the pause, Jackie continues, "I was so young and he was..." She sighs. "He was nothing to me."

"And now you feel guilty...Is this what you've been carrying around?"

She's crying again. I can hear her trying to pull the phone away from her face.

"Does Charlie know?"

"No."

"Why not?"

"Because…I don't know. Half of me is ashamed and the other half knows I did the right thing…I think…" A fresh round of tears comes through. "I…I think I feel guilty because I know I did the right thing."

"Then you did," I tell her quickly, with no room to spare before she crumbles again. "Listen to me, you are not being punished, Jackie. No one is punishing you. Shit happens equally to good people and bad—"

Being in journalism you see a lot of that. Unimaginable horrors happening to people who have the least to lose.

I think of Jake and everything he's endured. He's lost everyone he's ever been close to, everyone he's ever loved. And still he tries, despite what he's carrying around.

"This guilt is eating away at you, and it's not good for you or my niece. You need to talk to a professional… But I know this for a fact, tragedy doesn't discriminate. You didn't do anything to deserve those miscarriages. They just happened…Jack?" I prompt when all I get is silence.

"I'm nodding," she croaks.

"What about all the mistakes I've made? Don't you think I deserve to be happy despite them."

It makes me think of the day Ben fired me and what came before that. Dad was right, Halpern's family didn't deserve what I did to them.

In hindsight, had I not been in school and distracted by Halpern's story, I could've even been one of the journalists that speculated about Jake's guilt. Considering the circumstances, anyone would easily jump to the conclusion that Jake had been drinking that night. It would've been a fair assumption. "Assumptions make an ass out of you," Nan always says. And she's right, it would've been the wrong one.

"Of course, I do."

"Then what makes you different?" The silence is heavy and rife with trap doors. This could go either way so I nudge her in the right direction. "You are not your history any more than I am mine."

Or anymore than Jake is his, for that matter.

* * *

The next day I'm deep in the middle of researching on the annual Ironman competition hosted in July, which happens to be the second oldest Ironman in North America, when an email alert catches my attention.

It's from Sports Illustrated.

I open it and with every word I read, my level of

excitement soars. They want to do a feature story on Jake's organization and the kids. I can't keep a lid on it.

I jump into in the baby blue Mercedes and race to the farmhouse to spread the good news.

"Jake!" I shout, pushing through the front door. When he doesn't answer, I barrel down the hall.

"Jake?" I shout entering the studio.

He's staring at blank canvas. Just staring at it with an expression so pensive I almost forget why I came here.

In that moment I get another glimpse of what Jackie meant when she said she just knew. Because whether he likes it or not, Jake Turner is my once-in-a-lifetime love.

He turns to face me and a big smile stretches across his face. I get dimples and teeth and pure joy. "Come here."

I don't walk. I run. I run into his open arms. And he catches me.

Before he can kiss me I stop him. "I have to tell you something first." He nods. "Sports Illustrated wants to do a story on you and the boys."

His face falls. All of that good stuff I was getting from him a second ago is gone.

"No"

"Jake…I don't—"

"I can't do it, Carrie."

"Why?"

"Because I don't want to. The only reason I agreed to the Gazette is because it was local."

"I don't get it. You're doing an amazing thing for those boys. Why don't you want the world to know about it?"

"Because I just don't. That's why. Can't that be enough for you?"

It's the guilt. It's always the guilt. It's still there. Maybe it'll always be lurking beneath the surface.

"Jake, it was an accident." I can tell by his demeanor he's getting angry with me, but I press on. He can't live like this his entire life. "You can't keep punishing yourself like this. It's not healthy."

"Do you remember how bad things got for you after you posted that article?"

"Yeah," I answer, not certain where he's going with it.

"Multiply that times ten. Imagine people going through your entire life and trashing it. Twisting every single thing you've ever done to suit their agenda. Imagine the press standing outside your window for a year. Following you everywhere you go. Harassing the people you know. Drawing the wrong conclusions about everyone you're seen with…" He paces like a caged beast. "I do the S.I. article and it won't be about the kids. It'll be about me again. And Bresler and Karen and she doesn't deserve that."

I feel about two feet tall right now. He's right. I have no idea how bad he had it.

I hug his waist tightly and press my face into his chest, sniff the turpentine and soap. "I'm sorry I pushed. You're right… Sometimes I forget you're famous. To me you're just the hot guy that makes me come once a day."

He pushes back my shoulder's and looks down at me with nothing but trouble. "Once?"—his eyes narrow—"You better take that back."

Backpedaling, I head for the door. "One and a half when you try real hard."

He stalks after me. "I'm giving you one last chance to set the record straight."

I make it to the door. "Two at the very most."

"Start running now if you know what's good for you."

I take off and let him catch me on the couch. We rip each other's clothes off. And when I say we rip, I mean he breaks the strap of my overalls and I split his shirt in half.

Naked, I push him down and ride him until we're both sweaty and exhausted. Filled with pent up emotion, it takes everything I have left not to spill my guts.

I want to tell him how much he means to me. How much I love him. Because I do. I love him with all my heart and would never do anything to hurt him. But it won't come.

"Jake…"

He buries his face in my neck. And when we're done and he's holding me and kissing me, I take his face in my hands. "I promise I will never do anything to hurt you. I promise you."

Chapter Seventeen

It is a steadfast rule that when everything is going exceedingly well in your life something has to come along and carpet bomb it. Sometimes I wonder if the universe is allergic to happy people.

Things between Jake and me are so good it scares me. I am madly in love. I've never been this happy before. On the flip side, I'm petrified I'll be forced to choose between the man I love, or living the life I've always dreamed about. Seems unnecessarily cruel that God would make me choose.

We're getting a summer storm later tonight and a bank of clouds has started to crawl over the green mountain peaks on the other side of the lake. I'm working on the porch, busy piecing together the research on my new column for the week—this one on Songs at Mirror Lake, a free concert series coming up in July—when a burning need to tell Jake that I love him comes over me. Because really, what am I waiting for?

With the column only half done, I jump in the Nan's

Mercedes and take off for the farmhouse. They say the absence makes the heart grow fonder. I say anytime I'm not with him it's like a hole opens up in me so big I can hear the hollow sound of wind passing through, a constant hunger demanding to be fed. I say fonder is putting it lightly.

There's an unfamiliar car parked in the driveway next to the Expedition when I get there. A black Escalade, tinted windows, black hubcaps. My investigative mind starts working overtime. Jake didn't mention anyone coming to visit.

I'm about to reach for the handle of the front door when something tells me not to. My intuition rarely fails me, so I listen. Creeping around the side of the house, I hide behind a tree. And bingo.

Through the large picture window of his studio, I can see Jake half-seated on the stool. He's wearing the same faded Bears t-shirt I put on him this morning after we had sex in his shower. He smiles broadly, and my heart swells. Nothing makes me happier than seeing Jake smile because he does it so seldomly it feels like a gift.

Problem is, he's smiling at someone other than me. And not just someone, a woman.

The sense of betrayal I feel is devastating. My heart is

pounding so viciously it feels like it might explode inside my chest. And as I search why this pain feels so familiar when I've never been in love before, I realize it's the same feeling, the same pain I felt when my father told us my mother was never coming back.

Never in my life have I ever wanted to be more wrong. And yet my intuition never fails me.

Even though she has her back to the window, I can make out the shape of her. Long legs in skinny jeans, a perfect butt. She has muscle where I have none. She flips her curtain of straight red hair over her shoulder and turns sideways, revealing a face just as attractive as the rest of her. This is my basic nightmare.

When she places her hand on his shoulder, it takes everything I have not to charge in there and break those fingers off. Even worse, judging by their postures, it's clear as day that they know each other. Maybe an ex-girlfriend? Either way, I can't watch anymore.

Close to hyperventilating, I bend over to catch my breath. I almost can't believe it. If I wasn't seeing it for myself, I wouldn't believe it. And the thing is, it makes sense.

All the old feelings come storming back. I'm still that Pizza Face kid. And he'll always be a Stanley Cup winning hockey super star.

Two minutes later I hit the gas and the Mercedes' diesel engine clangs. The car rips down the driveway, kicking up gravel. The tears don't start until I hit 73 and head into town.

* * *

"Can I come in?"

Zelda looks back at me from behind the screen door of her rental. She's wearing white shorts, a gingham blouse, and a curious frown on her face.

I drove straight here from the farmhouse, then sat in the car for the past half hour hitting the reject button on my phone and crying my eyes out.

Zelda doesn't answer fast enough to satisfy my bad mood so I let her have it. "Are you serious right now?"

Her eyebrows quirk up. They haven't been done in a while and are growing bushy. I also note the beginnings of grey at her temple. This is a woman that used to sleep with fake eyelashes on, mind you. And not the cheap do-it-yourself kind. No, I'm talking the luxury salon variety that cost a fortune.

"I see you're going full country. That's commendable." The minute I say the words, I want to call them back. I'm not here to take shots at her. I'm here for answers.

"I'm sorry. I'm not here to insult you."

She pushes the door open and I march inside without sparing her a hello. I just can't right now.

"Would you like anything to drink?" she asks while I plant myself in a red Adirondack chair on her veranda overlooking the lake.

It's pretty out here. More populated since it's a stone's throw from town. A bunch of people are out on the lake canoeing even though the storm on the horizon is rolling in quickly, the sky grey and gloomy. It suits me. My mood is overcast with a chance of more tears.

"I'll take a Coke One if you have it...or anything diet."

"I have ginger ale," my mother replies. And isn't that just like her. She asks you what you want and then offers you something not even remotely similar.

"I'll pass. Thank you."

Zelda sashays outside with a glass of white wine in her hand and a smile in her hazel eyes. She takes a seat in the chair next to mine and sips her Chardonnay.

Meanwhile, I can't help my roaming attention. I'd forgotten how much we look alike. The same kneecaps, the same slim legs and narrow feet. Her toes are perfectly pedicured in coral polish. Mine in red. If I put my feet next to hers I probably couldn't tell much of a difference aside from the color of the toes.

Jackie looks exactly like my dad and I resemble Zelda. There's no denying it. It's my cross to bear.

My phone vibrates, and Jake's picture appears on screen. It's the fourth time he's called so I finally turn it off.

"Aren't you going to ask why I'm here?"

"No. I'm sure you'll get around to it."

If she thinks she's going to play doctor with me, she is sorely mistaken. "Please don't psychoanalyze me."

"I'm not, Carrie. I've asked to see you so we could talk at least a hundred times…" She sips her wine. "I'm done trying. You're not a hurt little kid anymore. You're an adult. You should start acting like one."

The top of my head practically explodes. "*I* should start acting like one? Are you kidding?" I scoff. "You've been running around town trying to hide your illicit affair with my father—"

"I wasn't *hiding* anything. I was keeping my word to your father. He wanted to break the news to you girls. I owe him that much."

"Oh, you owe all of us a lot more than that."

My mother tips her head back, closes her eyes, and takes a deep breath. "I don't want to fight with you."

Thing is, I don't want to fight either.

"Why? Why the sudden change? Why are you here?"

"I made a mistake, Carrie, and I'm trying to repair what I can."

"You can start by leaving dad alone."

"I won't. My relationship with your father is none of your business. Leaving him for Joan wasn't a mistake. And that's between your father and me.

"I don't owe you or your sister an explanation as to why I had to get out of my marriage. Nor do I regret living the life I wanted to live. I got a degree. I built a successful career. I'm proud of those achievements...The mistake I made was leaving you girls behind."

Between the farmhouse and this, I can't push any more emotions back down. They rise up and pour out of me. I wipe my damp cheeks with the back of my hand.

"I was ashamed," my mother says, her gaze faraway and directed at the ominous cloud cover. "I was ashamed so I ran away. I should've been strong enough to take you with me, but I wasn't. I felt like a caged animal given a taste of freedom and I had to protect that at all cost… unfortunately the cost was my children."

The silence lasts a good long time. It takes me that long to gather my thoughts and not lash out indiscriminately.

"I was mad at dad for a long time. I said terrible things to him because I thought you couldn't be the person everyone said you were. I defended you for years."

Everyday at school, I would wait at the curb, convinced that would be the day Zelda would return. My mother was famous for forgetting. Absentminded, my father called it. She would forget all the time to pick me up from ballet, from piano lessons, from day camp during the summer. I just accepted it.

So I thought it was only a matter of time before Zelda would drive up in her red Subaru Forrester, smiling her bright smile, take me in her arms and apologize. Then everyone would see that she didn't run away from us. That it was all a mistake. I would be vindicated and I would have my mom back.

Until one day my father got tired of getting calls from the school that I had once again missed the bus. That I was the last kid standing outside, waiting to be claimed like lost luggage.

He drove up that day and parked the car, waited for

me to get in and buckle my seatbelt. Then he told me what I was probably way too young to understand at the time. That every time my mom had forgotten to pick me up. It wasn't because I had slipped her mind. It was because she was with one of her lovers and I was the furthest thing from her thoughts. I never missed the bus again.

My mother wipes her own cheeks, no makeup to outline the tracks of tears falling down her face. "I can't change the past. I can't erase what I did. I can only apologize and do better now."

Something keeps needling me though. "Why now? We didn't hear from you for years. What's with the clothes and why are you suddenly changing everything about the life you say you loved."

"Life isn't a straight line, Carrie. People are entitled to change their minds. I needed a change...It was time for a change."

"Why now?"

The woman that gave birth to me turns to look me squarely in the eyes. "I have cancer."

* * *

Multiple Myeloma is a cancer of the bones. Life expectancy—four years. Though some live up to twenty.

I leave my mother's place under the pretext that I have plans with Jake. I tell her I'll be back and we can talk then. I've processed all that I can for today.

I don't know how to feel about her being ill and being back in town for good—according to her. But I know there's still a lot to resolve, a ton of hurt and mistrust on my end, and her being sick doesn't absolve her of any of that.

As I'm walking home, the heaven's decide to unleash hell. A carpet of anthracite grey clouds breaks open over me. And as if the pelting rain isn't bad enough, the lightening starts soon after that. In seconds, my Helmut Lang overall shorts and tank top are soaked, my red Pumas are squishy, and my buns are falling apart.

I'm halfway home when a set of headlights racing downhill pass me and stop. The barely distinguishable SUV pulls over to the side of the road and Jake gets out. "Carrie!" he yells from the other side as cars zip back and forth between us.

I keep walking because fuck him.

"Carrie! The hell are you doing!"

Picking up the pace, I glance over my shoulder to find him crossing the street and jogging after me. Naturally, I start to run. It takes all of a two seconds for him to catch up and throw me over his shoulder.

The screaming and pounding on his back do nothing to slow him down. He hauls me to the car and places me in the passenger seat. "Don't even think about getting out of this car," he barks, anger in his demeanor that no sane person would ever want to face down.

I wait until he gets in the driver's seat and pulls a U-turn to drive us back to the cottage.

"Have you lost your mind!" I'm so mad I can't even reply. Then the anger turns cold and the fight leaves me. "Why didn't you answer when I called?" he continues to hammer me.

"I don't have to do anything I don't want to," I calmly reply, staring out ahead.

Jake parks in the spot in front of the Austen and turns the engine off. The rain falling harder than ever, it's a sheet of solid water on the windshield.

"What is going on? Everything was fine this morning, and now you won't speak to me?" A pause. "Are you on the rag?"

That gets a reaction. I turn to look at him with what is definitely murder in my eyes. His hair is soaked and slicked back, his eyes wild with confusion and anger.

"You're an asshole."

He jerks back, surprise written on his face. "I'm the asshole? I am? How am I the asshole? Explain that to me. I find you walking home in the middle of a thunderstorm and you won't speak to me, but *I'm* the asshole—"

"I came to see you! I was at the farmhouse today. I saw her, Jake—the redhead. I saw her. So yeah, you are the asshole."

He blinks. Blinks again. The beads of water on his lashes are making them stick together and appear thicker and darker. No man should be that lucky.

His mouth quivers. "You were at the farmhouse?"

"Isn't that what I said?" I snap.

He bites his bottom lip, his white teeth looking brighter in contrast to his beard.

"Around four?"

"Yes, Sherlock. Around four."

He makes a sound between a snort and a sigh. "But you didn't come inside. Instead, you decided to play *investigative reporter...*" The mocking tone is not doing him any favors. He's not even denying it. I'm wrecked. "Instead, you spied on me."

"I'm getting out."

"The hell you are," he fires back rather angrily. "Sit your ass down and listen."

"You have some nerve—"

"—That was the daughter of the owner of the Chicago Blackhawks that you saw me with."

Huh? Is that supposed to make me feel better?

When he sees the blank look on my face, he exhales tiredly. "They want me to play for them."

Oh. A sinking sensation comes over me.

"Why was she at your house?"

"Because I've turned down their offer twice and they thought making a pitch in person would make a difference. Autumn is the GM…the general manager of the team."

"I know what a GM is thank you very much."

Jake tried to school a grin. We stare at each other, neither one of us wanting to be the first to look away.

"Come here," he murmurs.

Soaking wet and looking like hell, I crawl out of my seat and straddle his lap, place my forehead against his equally soaked neck.

Jake wraps his arms, warm and secure, around me, pets my back, gently untangles my hair. All the while my insides wrestle between hysterical laughter and shame.

And love. So much love I can barely contain it all. "I'm sorry."

He hums. "Don't ever quit talking to me, okay? If you have a problem, tell me."

I nod. And just when I think I can't possibly love this man anymore than I already do, he makes a liar out of me.

Chapter Eighteen

"What's on the agenda today?" I ask, sipping one of the lattes I made for us.

Jake gives me a knowing smile that means I'm not getting any information out of him. Then he spoons Cheerios in a mouth made pink by all the kissing we're doing lately.

Love is one powerful drug.

I never thought I would find a half naked man eating cereal drop dead sexy and yet here he is. I'm staring at arguably the sexiest man on the planet, wearing nothing but black boxer briefs and casually leaning back against the counter with a bowl in his hand.

I would never say this out loud, but every time I look at him I can't believe he's mine. I mean—not mine per se. I know this is temporary. I'm not living in a fictional world. Eventually, we'll part ways. The problem starts when I think of us actually parting ways. Then I get sick to my stomach.

The Blackhawks want him badly. They haven't given

up trying to get him either. Since the GM showed up in town a few weeks ago, he gets a *just checking in* call with more dollars attached every week.

I have a sneaking suspicion Jake wants to take the offer too.

"All you need to know is that we're going on a hike. I took care of everything else. Equipment, boots everything…"

"Equipment? Hmm, sounds serious."

He puts the bowl down in the sink, wipes his hands and mouth on a paper napkin, and walks up to where I'm standing at the other end of the small kitchenette.

Taking the cup out of my hand, he places it down on the table. Then he picks me up and places me on the counter. His face snuggles against the side of my neck as he steps between my legs. It didn't take long for us to figure out each other's likes and needs. There is also something to be said about practice.

My hands instinctively rise to cup his head and my short nails rake through his hair. He sighs contentedly, and I do it again.

I knew Jake would be a great lover, I just never expected him to be so affectionate. So willing to give affection and comfort, and so desperate to receive it. It makes my heart ache for what he missed out on as a kid.

"You need a haircut," I tell him, kissing his temple and making lazy figure eights against the dense pile of dark brown hair. "I can't believe how fast your hair grows."

"I need you," he mutters against my skin, the feeling heightened by the rasp of his voice and the kisses that follow.

There's always the slightest edge of desperation in the way Jake makes love to me. As if he doesn't seize what he wants right this minute, he may never get it, the latter being completely intolerable to him.

Cupping my butt, he pulls me closer to the edge of the counter and steps between my legs, pressing his body against mine. "This is for you," he murmurs, flexing his hips.

As if we hadn't already made love this morning at the break of dawn and once again in the shower.

Only our underwear and my oversized t-shirt separate us, and yet the clothes only serve to heighten the sensation. He flexes his hips again, and I almost come from that alone. "Only you…" I feel the gentle scrape of teeth where his lips have been.

Pushing against me, he sets a steady rhythm, and

before long, I am seconds from going off. "Don't come yet," he growls.

I barely remember my first name and he wants me to follow orders? "I'm coming," I warn him.

Shoving down his boxers, he yanks my underwear aside and enters me—the scream torn from my chest as I come.

Holding me tightly, both of us breathing heavy, Jake waits for me to finish to start moving in a wickedly lazy rhythm intended to drive me insane. It's controlled and steady, and exactly what my body needs to reboot and begin the slow climb back up to free fall.

"Jake…Jake…" His name means all things to me. Love and friendship and everything good. Everything I've been looking and hoping for. And since I can't say any of that. Since I can't tell him how I feel. I say his name.

Digging my heels into his bubble butt, I urge him on. And being generous to a fault, he does. He gives it to me. He lets go of his vaunted control and gives me everything he's got. And when he comes, I do too. We do it together. Two loners who found someone to need.

* * *

"Is this supposed to be fun? Give me a head's up

when we get to the fun part," I say, wheezing.

We've been hiking up the mountain for the better part of two hours and according to the man I am madly in love with, we've got one more to go. "Seriously?" He's not listening to me, his bubble butt keeps moving up the steep incline. Thank God for hockey butt; at least the view is worth it. "Jake! I need to stop and check some stuff…for work."

"You're not checking Twitter."

"I am. It's my job."

He chuckles, but at least he stops and turns. "That is not your job. Your job is to write. Twitter is for a bunch of people with a ton of anger who want someone to take it out on without ending up in divorce court or with a restraining order."

He's not wrong. "Yeah, but it's good for business, you cynic."

My feet can't do it anymore. I sit my ass down on a flat rock, take off my backpack, fish out my water bottle and, you guessed it, my phone. "Some of us like to be part of society. But you go on ahead, Captain America. I'll catch up in a bit."

"There are black bears all over this mountain."

"Then come back here and protect me."

"Told you it wouldn't hurt to build a little muscle." He smirks.

"I am building muscle. I get a serious work-out *at least* twice a day now. Coached by a world-class athlete… although I'm not fond of his attitude right now."

He walks over, watching as I lift my arm up to try and catch a signal. One second later, I no longer have a phone because I watch it soar through the air in a gentle arc and land in a deep gorge.

I scream. "My phone!!"

"I'll get you another one."

I am in shock. Barely able to breathe. Jake leans down and kisses me. When I don't kiss him back because I'm in shock, he kisses me again.

"Tomorrow," I growl. "The second we get back. You're buying me a new one."

He chuckles drily and takes a pull of his water. Meanwhile, I'm in deep, deep mourning for my phone.

Looking over the mountain range, Jake's expression gets suddenly serious. "You can't get this in L.A."

He's right about that. The beauty of this place always does take me by surprise. I don't know why. I grew up here. It wasn't all bad. There are horse drawn sleigh rides during Christmas and the most spectacular fireworks in

July. There's clean air and soul inspiring vista's like this one.

"Yeah, but you don't have the Getty Museum and sushi on the Sunset Strip at midnight. You don't have the Hollywood Bowl and Malibu Cove."

He turns to search my face. "And you can't live without sushi at midnight?"

I swallow, knowing full well what he means. I can live without sushi at midnight. I can live without all of it, but I'm pretty sure I can't live without him.

"Depends…"

"Ready to keep going?"

I nod. This is more than a hike, this is us on the precipice of something big.

Jake offers an outstretched hand while I gaze at the intricate pattern tattoo on his forearm. It's as familiar to me now as my own arm. We climb the rest of the way with very little talking, both of us reserving our energy. Or maybe it's the knowledge that it's time to put our cards on the table.

My column is gaining readers every day and the Blackhawks want him desperately. How long can we continue to live in this bubble of bliss without the outside world sneaking in.

"This is it," he says when we finally reach a clearing at the top of a peak.

Jake slides his sunglasses to the top of his head and looks over his shoulder at me with a spark in his eyes. He drops his much heavier backpack and comes over to take mine.

From this vantage point you can see all three lakes with crystal clarity. The sun is so strong at this altitude that I can't even take off my sunglasses. Ducking my head, I blink to give my eyes a rest and spot a small flat rock a few feet away. There's writing on it. Faded. Barely legible.

I love you always.

"I've thought a lot about what you said—about your grand adventure."

My attention snaps back to the man I love, my guts fluttering with nerves.

"When I was living in the projects with my mother I used to collect plastic bottles and cans for money. We needed it, but it was more than that. It was a way to keep my mind busy. A lot of the kids in my building were into some bad shit and my mother never like me hanging with them…anyway, after my contract with the Bears, I traveled a lot in the off-season. Thailand, Italy, Norway. I guess I was looking for a grand adventure too." His earnest gaze meets mine. "But you know what…" He shakes his head. "It was no better than hunting for those bottles.

"I love you. I love you so much it scares the shit out of me. But I won't be the guy that holds you back from doing what you want…I think loving someone means you let them make their own choices. When I told you at the rink that I wanted all those things for you, and you thought I was making fun of you"—he shakes his head—"I wasn't."

A second of silence passes and then I can't wait any longer. I march up to him and throw my arms around his waist. "I love you too."

* * *

We set up camp and eat dinner. I packed sandwiches. By nightfall, we're exhausted and tuck in early, both of us in one giant sleeping bag.

"Where did you get this thing," I ask as I inspect it.

"Amazon."

I laugh and laugh. And Jake kisses me. He kisses me like he loves me. And I kiss him back like I love him more. Peeling my leggings and underwear down, he touches me between my legs with skilled fingers that make art so beautiful it makes me cry. Before long, I'm screaming my orgasm into a night sky littered with a million stars. The magic of the moment not captured in something artificial, but forever branded in my mind.

Taking me by the hips, he positions me facing away and pulls me back against his erection, hard and hot against my skin. "This good," he says.

It's all good. Everything with him is good. How could I possibly give it up?

He enters me from behind, his hand under my thermal, over my breast. His mouth near my ear.

"I love you," he murmurs over and over as he pumps into me.

"Jake," I cry out as I come. And when we're done and he's holding me and I'm so happy tears are running down my face. I whisper, "I love you always."

* * *

"Let's go, Anderson."

This hike has kicked my ass. Ironically, I'm moving a lot more slowly going down the mountain, than I was going up.

"Can we stop?"

"We've got one hour left." He turns to check me out. "Call mercy if you want."

I'm not calling mercy. No way. He'll use that against me forever…or at least as long as we're together. Which I hope is forever.

I'm not even going to kid myself—if I had to choose between him and the life. I'll choose him. I'd choose him every single time.

"Babe…do you want to play again?"

He stops finally. Had I known that was the password I would've used it hours ago.

He turns and looks at me, shrugs. "A year ago I would've answered no. But…"

"But now you do."

He nods once. My suspicion was correct.

"What are you going to do about it?"

Gaze cast down. "I don't know…I don't know."

"Can I ask you something else?"

"Anything."

"A few months ago I watched the game, the Stanley Cup against the Penguins." His face gets tight. It's his defensive face. I know it well by now. "Did you get a concussion from that hit you took in the third period?"

The look on his face has my fine tuned reporter's antenna sounding the alarm that I'm over the target. "You were punched in the face. I saw the tape, Jake. Did they check you for a concussion?"

Jake blinks, expression neutral. It's a dead giveaway.

"You did."

He starts walking down the mountain again.

"Jake? Jake!" I run after him. Grabbing his wrist, I stop him and he lets me. "Talk to me. You said we would always talk this out. So talk to me. You had a concussion that night…why did you drive?"

His shoulders fall. Turning, he faces me. "I had a concussion that night. Which is why I didn't party in the locker room with everyone else."

"Then why did you drive?"

It takes him forever to answer. "I didn't…I wasn't driving that night. Mike was."

I don't think he could've said anything more shocking. I want to ask a million questions and nothing is coming out of my mouth.

"Mike was driving?" He looks off and nods. "Mike was driving and crashed…why?"

"The police fucked it up and I didn't correct them. My blood came back clean and Mike's was above the legal limit. It…it just made everything easier."

I bend over, hands on my knees, and take a deep breath—on the verge of hyperventilating while Jake rubs my back.

"We had just won the Cup. It was easier for the team…for Karen to get Mike's life insurance payout. If he had died with drugs and alcohol in his system and he was driving, the policy was void."

"But it wasn't easier for you."

"Mike had a lot of debt."

"So you got screwed." He makes a face. "You're lucky to be alive. Mike could've killed you both…" I am so mad for him right now I want to resurrect that bastard so I can strangle him.

"Babe…"

"Mike was good to me. He was my best friend. I couldn't let him down."

"Jake…" Reaching up, I take his face in my hands. "He let you down. All he had to do was ask, and the airport would've gotten you a driver."

"It is what it is."

He pulls my hands away from his face and starts walking again. Neither one of us says a word the rest of the hike.

Chapter Nineteen

"Darling!"

There's only one person that calls me that and that same person also has a slight British accent.

Ben is sitting on the porch of the Austen when Jake and I return from our hike. He stands, beaming at me, looking handsome in a white linen shirt with the sleeves rolled up to the elbows and designer jeans.

I would have preferred him to look haggard and pale but no, he's looking as fit as ever with a deep tan and slightly longer hair.

"I've been waiting all day."

In contrast, Jake and I walk up looking sunburnt and as worn-out as a dollar bill in a strip club. Ben's line of sight moves over to Jake. Lifting his aviator sunglasses, he gives Jake the once-over and declares him a non-issue. This man's arrogance knows no boundaries.

"What are you doing here?" My tone communicates exactly how I feel about the subject.

Jake walks past me, checks Ben out, and says, "First-best," to me. Which makes me feel like crap. He needs me right now, more than ever, and instead I have to deal with Ben.

Love truly is blind because now that they're standing next to each other, I don't know what I was thinking. There's no comparison. Ben is a faded image in contrast to Jake's bright, shiny colors.

"Jake, wait…"

"Come get me when you're done," he tells me without a backward glance. I watch him walk into the Hemingway looking more than a little bruised.

"What do you want Ben?"

He looks over his shoulder at the door behind which the love of my life disappeared. "Boyfriend trouble?"

"No trouble at all. So, to what do I owe this visit?"

Ben plays with the stem on his sunglasses. "I'm at ABC now."

"Good for you."

"I need you on my team."

"No," I tell him right off.

"Is there anywhere we can talk?"

If I don't do this now, and do it decisively, it will never end. "Inside," I say pointing to the Austen.

Ben follows me, glancing around while I go to the

kitchen and get myself a tall glass of water. "Anything to drink? I have Diet Coke and Coke One. Pick your poison."

"No, thank you. I had lunch in town."

"You came a long way for nothing."

"I'm prepared to make a very generous offer, Carrie. You can write your own ticket. Anything you want."

"Anything?" I say leaning against the doorframe of the kitchenette sipping my water.

"Anything."

"I want you to take no for an answer."

Ben sobers, his smile fading quickly. "Are we negotiating? Is that what this is?"

"Jesus…I don't remember you being this willfully thick. I'm not coming back. Not for all the rubies in the world. I have a good thing going here. I have my own column with the Gazette and there's a good chance it'll get syndicated."

"I've read your column. It's…sweet and…entertaining but—"

"But what?" All the old feelings of inadequacy come back. The rented mule syndrome. For so many years, I looked up to Ben and thought he hung the moon. It's a knee-jerk reaction to want him to think well of my work.

"It's not you. You're hard news and breaking scandals. You're not charities for kids and old ladies that play...what do you call that sport with the brooms and the pots of stone. Really stupid sport—"

"Curling. And trust me, it's harder than it looks."

"I'll take your word for it."

I breathe a sigh of relief. "Thanks, Ben."

He smiles again. It's his sly, victory smile. I've seen it a million times. "We'll work out the details when you get to L.A."

"Oh, I'm not coming back. I'm thanking you for making it easier. You just insulted my work and simultaneously made me realize that *breaking scandals* is not my thing anymore. So thank you, Ben, for helping to make the most important decision of my life an easy one."

"You're not coming back, are you?"

"No."

Nodding, Ben looks around. "I have nowhere to stay for the night." He sounds positively downtrodden. I'm getting way too much satisfaction out of this. "Do you think I could stay here? I have a 6 a.m. flight to LaGuardia."

I have a man waiting for me next door.

"Lock the door on your way out tomorrow."

* * *

There are times in life when one should exercise caution. This isn't one of those times.

"I choose you," I say to the man I love as soon as I step foot in the Hemingway.

Freshly showered, he's in bed reading a book on child psychology. I'm pretty sure that was the sound of my uterus exploding.

He looks up and runs his eyes over me. I'm still in my hiking clothes, my cheekbones on the dark side of crispy, and I probably smell. Suddenly, I'm rethinking my grand entrance.

"Ben?"

"He's staying the night and leaving tomorrow early—for good…I'm not going back to L.A. He was offering me everything I ever wanted and I said no." I laugh. "I thanked him. I actually thanked the arrogant prick. He made me realize that everything I want is here…the column. You…Mostly you."

"Come here," he says, putting the book down.

Shaking my head. "Let me take a shower first."

Jake gets out of bed and stalks toward me. Taking me in his arms, he picks me up and carries me into the bathroom where he undresses me. In the shower, he washes my body and hair, runs his big capable hands over ever inch of me while I return the favor.

He makes love to me in the shower like he's pouring out his soul. And when he's done, I pour out mine. "I want to scream it to the world that you weren't driving that night, that it's not your fault that Mike is dead. That he was the irresponsible one…but I won't. I love you, and if this is what you want, then I'll carry it with you… you don't have to carry this alone anymore."

* * *

Three days later the proverbial poop hits the fan. I'm driving into town, to go food shopping, when I notice a long line of black SUVs driving around. No big deal. We get a ton of VIPs and the summer music festival has started. It's days away from the Fourth of July.

My feelers, however, go up when I start to see news trucks from local stations parked all along Main Street.

I grab a few items that I need and forgo the rest. I need to get back to the Cottages as quickly as possible and snoop around to see if I can find out what this is about. Who knows, maybe Martha Stewart is in town or something.

I head for the kitchen, which is where I find Dad. He

looks at me funny. "Have you seen Jake?"

Strange question. It's just past noon. Jake usually paints until sundown. Unless it's a Tuesday or Thursday, like today, then he's coaching the kids, in which case he gets done around five.

Regardless, Dad's got me worried now so I text him. Five minutes later, still no response. This is out of the ordinary. Jake always answers a text. He's never not answered a text. I try to call but it goes straight to voicemail without ringing. He's turned his phone off. My heart starts beating super fast, that old intuition telling me this is not a drill.

"I'm going to the rink. It's a coaching day. Call me if he shows up here," I tell my father and jump into the Mercedes.

All my fears are realized when I get to the Arena. The parking lot is swarming with news trucks and unmarked vehicles. Parking at the curb, I run to the door and have to fight a crowd of reporters six rows deep.

"Hey, they're not letting anybody in," one of them hollers at me.

"I'm a hockey mom," I yell back.

The doors are locked. I bang and bang but I can't see a soul. My anxiety level peaks at this point.

"What story are you guys all here for?" I ask one bleached blonde reporter once I escape the scrum.

"Pro hockey player. He was a really big deal a few years ago. One of the best. New evidence just emerged that he wasn't driving the car that killed his teammate. The guy that died was."

Oh fuck oh fuck oh fuck oh fuck.

I jump in the Mercedes and tear out of the parking lot, headed straight for the farmhouse. His Expedition isn't in the driveway like it normally is, but I suspect he parked it in the garage to avoid detection. In fact, there isn't a news van in sight.

The front door is locked so I go around the back. Again, no luck. I spy through the windows and see no one is home.

Dejected and riddled with anxiety, I get back in the car and call him again. It goes straight to voicemail. Either he doesn't want to talk, or he doesn't want to talk to me. Either way it sucks.

I'm distraught on the drive back home. Somehow, I know this is my fault. Maybe it was the article on the boys. Maybe it was someone at S.I. who decided to dig deeper into the details of the police report. Who knows. But I need to see him and speak to him. I need to make sure he's okay.

I grab my laptop out of the Austen and go check the Hemingway as soon as I get back to Comfort Cottages, knowing that I would find it empty.

Falling into bed, I sniff the pillow that carries Jakes scent. I miss him already and I have no idea where he's gone.

I turn on the computer and that's when I see it in the banner at Yahoo. ABC breaking story and Jake's picture. He's dressed in all black, including his sunglasses. It must be Mike's funeral because his arm is around a woman who's crying. She too is dressed in black. I click on the article and my eyes go immediately to the author.

Ben Hall.

Chapter Twenty

For two consecutive days I stay in the Hemingway waiting for him. All his clothes are here. He's got to come get them at some point. I've called a million times, but the call either goes directly to voicemail or rings twice and goes to voicemail. I'm so worried I haven't shed a single tear. A wall of ice has formed around me and nothing can get out.

On the Fourth of July, Gina convinces me to come to the park for fireworks. In reality, I refuse vehemently, but she doesn't take no for an answer. Her little red BMW comes buzzing up the hill and she honks and honks until I'm forced to get dressed and join her.

"What are you doing here," I ask Gray when I see him in the back seat of the car.

He smiles tightly. "Moral support."

I get in and buckle up. Turn to my friend and admire her flawless makeup and even more flawless life. "You two are together, aren't you?"

"No," says Gina at the same time Gray says, "Yes."

"Which is it?"

"Yes," says Gina at the same time Gray says, "No."

At the park, among the hundreds of families and couples lounging on blankets laid out all over the field, I hit rock bottom. I've never felt so alone in my life. Then it gets worse. By some strange coincidence, I spot my parents in the crowd. My father leans down and kisses my mother.

I want to scream. I want to cry and throw a tantrum. I had love. I had the love of the best man I have ever known or will ever know and I screwed it up. Because that's what I do. I get carried away and screw things up.

For the next three hours, I suffer through some of the most spectacular fireworks I've ever seen. There's something intrinsically romantic about fireworks, which of course reminds me of Jake.

Then I have to suffer through Gray holding Gina's hand and kissing every single one of her fingertips. They gave up trying to hide it as soon as we got out of the car. It reminds me of Jake. Because everything reminds me of Jake.

By 9 p.m. all I want to do is crawl under Jake's sheets and breath in his scent. I've been doing that on the regular lately, taking hits every couple of hours just to get a piece of him.

Nobody warns you about the withdrawal symptoms. Nobody tells you that detox is more excruciatingly painful than never having known how wonderful real love is.

When Gina drops me off, the lights in the Hemingway are on. My feet can't carry me fast enough. I race to the threshold of the open door and find him inside. Jake is back—and he's throwing stuff in his luggage.

"Jake…" My voice is so weak and shaky I barely recognize it as my own.

He pauses the packing and looks at me. His face is blank, remote. I hardly recognize him. At least when he was Scrooge there was some emotion there. This version of Jake, I don't know. He's retreated so far back, I'm petrified I may never reach him again.

"I didn't do it."

"He knew every detail." He shakes his head. "Doesn't matter. It's done. I'm leaving. I'm checking out. I'm paid up until August so we're good, yeah?"

He throws the rest of his work-out clothes in the bag. All black. Sneakers. Sweatpants. Track pants. Underwear. He's wearing black now. For a man who's so good with color, he doesn't care for it in his life.

I take a step closer and he zips up the bag. "Don't come any closer."

He sounds so cold, so remote, I stop in my tracks. My heart is beating as fast as a rabbit caught in a trap. I swallow down the fear and sense of loss, but it does nothing to stop the tears running down my face. And once they start, they continue unchecked.

"Please hear me out."

"I've been doing damage control for the past five days…It's over, Carrie," he says, without sparing me a single glance.

"Jake. You know me. I love you. You know I would *never*, ever do anything to hurt you."

"I know nothing." His chin lifts and his gaze meets mine. It's completely shuttered. "I know I told you something no one else on the planet knew, and now it's everywhere."

Grabbing the overstuffed duffle bag, he walks past me without touching or looking at me. Like I'm beneath contempt. He doesn't even pause by the door. He walks right out of my life as if he'd never been the best part of it.

* * *

"Are you sure?" Hal looks like he's in physical pain.

"No. But I've got to get out of here and I'll listen to what they have to say."

The Huffington Post made me an offer. It's nowhere near as good as Ben's was. However, the Post isn't a rat sucking traitor like Ben is.

I figured out how Ben broke the story. Ben did not break the story...I did.

We rented out the Hemingway a few days after Jake checked out. The new Mr. and Mrs. Elmendurst liked to have vigorous sex in the shower. I heard every single word of their dirty talk from the other side of the wall.

So in the end, Jake was right. It was all my fault.

I'm going back to Cali tomorrow. I can't stay here now. Too many reminders. Maybe it's for the best. If love is so fragile, probably best to stay away.

"Sorry about the column."

Hal smiles. "Don't worry about the column, but listen here...I'm gettin' old and tired. One of these days I'm going to retire and nothing would give me more pleasure than to hand the keys over to you."

I'm crying again. I've been doing a lot of that lately. "I'll think about it."

I swing by **Queen** to say goodbye to Gina. As if I

haven't shed enough tears already, her and I exchange a few more.

"I really think he's going to come to his senses soon."

She doesn't know Jake like I do. The man is an iron curtain when he wants to be. "No, G. He's not."

Back at the main house, I find my mother sitting outside on the veranda, reading a book.

"Mind if I sit?"

Glancing up, she lifts her sunglasses and smiles. "I would love for you to sit," she tells me. "Have you heard from him?"

I shake my head. "No. He's very stubborn. It's probably one of the reasons he's so successful at everything he does."

"Yes, he's quite impressive."

"And he did it all on his own…foster kid."

We sit in silence for a while looking out at the lake. It's a comfortable kind of silence. Seems like being in each others company is getting easier each day. All the turbulence gone. "When does it get easier?"

"Are you asking your mother or are you asking Dr. Zelda Anderson?"

It takes me a minute to answer. "I'm asking my mother."

"The time it takes to heal is the measure of the love you give."

In that case I'll never be over him.

"You may not want to hear this, but you are so much like me in so many ways…your exuberance, your love of the chase…but the love you give, the size of your heart… that's all your dad."

I wipe the dampness from my cheeks and swallow.

"Be patient with yourself. Let yourself feel it. You'll know when it's done. And then it will be done for good."

The next morning, Nan waits for me on the porch steps while Dad loads my luggage.

"Goodbye Elvis you sicko." I pet his massive head and he hisses. "Bye Nan, love you." I kiss her weathered cheek, sniff the combination of cigarettes and Shalimar, and she slips a check in my hand. Gene and Zelda drive me to the airport. On the way, I glance at Nan's check. Twenty thousand dollars. I'm shocked and grateful and sad at the same time. I'm always sad now. At the gate, I hug them both and promise to visit soon. The whole thing seems less weird every day.

On the plane, I link up the wifi and do what I have resisted doing for weeks. I Google him. He's given two interviews. Bob Costas and some woman I don't recognize. Maybe a Canadian reporter. He looks so handsome, all polished and primped. His hair perfect, the beard trim. The suit impeccable.

But it's the vacant look in his eyes as he explains to Costas that he did it to protect the memory of his best friend that breaks my heart.

Nobody deserves to be loved and worshiped more than Jake does. He's had so little of it in his life and all he does is keep trying to give it away. I contemplate writing him an email, but all I do is cause him pain. It's probably best I stay out of his life.

* * *

"I look like a beached whale. Just say it," Jackie says as soon as I step in the house. Charlie puts down my bags and goes to give her a kiss.

"Nah, you look like someone who's ready to squirt a baby out soon."

"Ew, that gross."

Five days later, Jackie waddles into the pool house and grunts as she falls into the couch. "I'm so happy you're here," she says, shoveling ice cream into her mouth while we binge watch *Euphoria*. "You have no idea how much I missed you. I almost made Charlie go fetch you like five times."

She's been very sentimental lately.

"Well good thing you almost got me killed for nothing," I mutter. Jackie starts bawling and I start laughing. "I'm kidding! Jeez. This poor kid of yours. I feel bad for her."

If it wasn't for Jackie, I would've never met Jake.

"Have you tried calling him again?"

I've had a lot of time to think lately.

"No...I'm done trying. If he believes that I would do that to him, then I don't know if we ever really stood a chance."

Jackie nods pensively and doesn't argue. Jackie is the most pragmatic person I know. If she thinks I'm doing the right thing by staying away, then it's probably the right thing to do.

* * *

"Carrie! Jackie is going into labor prematurely! We're headed to Cedar Sinai. Meet us there!"

The call came in when I was interviewing with Kate at the Huff Post and I sent it straight to voicemail.

Charlie sounds panicked. Charlie has never been anything other than chill since the day I met him an eternity ago, which means there must be something legitimate to panic about. It sends me into full-tilt hysteria.

I run around the underground parking garage of the building where the Huff Post is located like an inmate released from prison for CoVid. Right now, I have zero recollection where I parked Jackie's Land Rover.

After wasting a good twenty minutes, a security officer takes pity on me and comes to my rescue with his golf cart. By then, my sister's Stella McCartney blouse is soaked in sweat, and my hair (that Jackie insisted I leave down) is a Colombian necktie wrapped around my neck.

When did it get so unbearably hot in L.A.? I don't remember it being this freaking hot. Somehow while contemplating the heat, I start longing for cold winter nights and snowstorms. There's something seriously wrong with me.

By the time I get to the hospital, Jackie is in labor. I take a hold of her hand while Charlie is on the other side, but after the baby's heart rate spikes the doctor tells her it's time for a C-section.

They take my sister away and I send up a silent prayer to keep her safe. On my left, Charlie is crying.

* * *

"I know I'm just another silly parent, but I swear this is the most beautiful child ever to be created," Jackie croons with a broad smile on her face.

She's high as a kite on endorphins. She must be because I don't remember her ever looking so peaceful. It seems like Jackie did more than give birth to a perfect baby girl. It looks like she killed some demons in the process as well.

Watching my sister with her daughter makes me realize everything I thought I wanted pales in comparison. Because this…this is it. Loving and being loved. Giving and receiving it is everything.

I miss Jake so much tears funnel down my face. Jackie turns from watching Athena's small sleeping face in her arms and when she sees the tears, she smiles. "I don't want her to be her history. I want her to be bold and brave."

"And when she screws up?"

"Tomorrow is another day to get it right."

Brushing the dampness away from my cheeks, I nod.

"What are you doing here?"

I make a face. "Celebrating the birth of my niece, you dunce. What do you think?"

"I mean, what are you doing here, Carrie?"

Nothing meaningful. The tears start falling again at the same time Charlie walks in. He takes one look at the two of us, mutters something to the effect of, "Sisters," and walks out.

"Go get him."

"He thinks I leaked the story to Ben."

Jackie makes a face. "Convince him otherwise."

"I don't think I can."

Jackie eventually falls asleep and Charlie conks out in the chair next to her. These two help me keep the faith that maybe one day I'll be as lucky. I can only hope.

It's almost ten when I get back to the house in Pacific Palisades. I pull into the driveway, ready to hit the garage door opener, when a large figure sitting on the front steps of the house stands.

He's dressed in black track pants and a zip up hoody. A large duffel bag is hanging from his hand. I would know the shape of that man from sixty feet in a snowstorm.

Everything comes bubbling to the surface at once: love, pain, regret, the hurt. My hearts begins to race with a mix of love and anxiety.

Parking the Land Rover, I step out and Jake gives me the smallest of smiles. He walks over to the car and stops right in front of me. His gaze moving over my face like he can't believe his lying eyes.

"Hi." Then a deep sigh.

I can barely answer. "Hi…what are you doing here?"

"Can we talk…inside?"

I nod because, unlike him, I give people the benefit of the doubt. Especially someone I love.

He walks into the pool house, glancing around. "Nice place."

"What are you doing here, Jake?" Now that he's here acting sheepish all I am is angry.

"I came to see you."

"It's been a month."

He nods. "Yeah, I know."

"You walked out and you wouldn't let me explain."

"I know."

Frustration builds and soon I can feel the tears rising up, trying to break loose.

"I loved you. I loved you more that I have ever loved anyone and you wouldn't even listen! You said we would always talk and the first sign of trouble you cut and run."

He's nodding, gaze cast down. "I know. I'm sorry…I never let myself love anybody. Not after my mother. But then Mike grew on me. He wouldn't leave me alone. He forced me to be his friend…and then he died. And I was alone again.

"Then you came along and I…" He huffs. "I liked you right away. I didn't think I deserved anyone like you, but I couldn't stop wanting you. I just...Everyone I loved died…so I tried to…"

He exhales sharply. "…I think I was waiting for the shoe to drop on us for so long that when the story broke, I thought that was it."

I watch him chew on the inside of his cheek. "I was scared of losing you…and I was tired of being scared…I love you, Carrie. No matter what happens here. You have to know that." He takes two deep breaths. "I will love you with everything I am for the rest of my life. And if there is any chance that you could love me again, will you let me try?"

He looks so utterly lost, stripped bare, that I can't hold onto my hurt feelings for a second longer.

"Come here," I tell him.

He takes one slow step toward me. Then another. And another. Until his arms are around me and mine are around him. I take a deep breath of his chest, get on my toes and breathe in the skin of his neck.

I don't need to waste a lifetime to figure out what I already know. It's all meaningless without someone to share the triumphs and the screw-ups.

Yes, Jake screwed-up. But then again, so have I.

"It was my fault," I confess, because fair is fair.

"It doesn't matter."

"Not purposely. He heard us talking—when he stayed overnight at the cottage."

"It doesn't matter." Hugging me tighter, he kisses the top of my head.

"I love you too. You're my once-in-a-lifetime, Turner. What are we going to do about that?"

He exhales deeply and I can hear the relief in it. "There are things I can change—like where I live—and things I can't. And how I feel about you is one of them. I'll get us a house tomorrow. All you have to do is say the word."

Glancing up at him, I say the words I could never have anticipated in my wildest dreams. "I want to go home."

A flicker of joy replaces the relief on his face. "Really?"

"Really."

Epilogue

There are fish under my feet. I wiggle my toes and some try to mouth the glass. Technically, they're tropical fish and—

"Is that a baby shark!" I yelp, more than a little alarmed.

My husband walks over and peers down at the glass tile floor in our over-the-water bungalow. Glancing up, he smiles and places a brief kiss on my lips.

"Bathing suit, Carebear. Get it on or we'll be late for our dive."

I'm suddenly feeling less than excited. "Do I have to?"

"Grand adventure." He fights a smile.

"Yeah, but…"

Never have I eaten my words like I have with this man. I've invoked the mercy rule more times than I'd care to admit.

We celebrated my birthday in Patagonia. His at Machu Picchu. We've eaten breakfast in London and gone to sleep in Dubai. It's been four years of non-stop adventures. But the best adventure of all by a million miles has been the two of us at home on the lake during the off-season. Quiet nights debating the merits and detriments of the European Union, sharing books, and stories.

Jake was right. I didn't have to live in a big city to live a life worth writing about. I just had to live the one I had to the fullest, in the moment, and not always in anticipation of something better around the corner.

Hal retired and handed the Gazette over to me and Gray. I, in turn, handed the Editor In Chief job to Gray. It's a funny thing, finally getting what you want—in my case it was recognition for my work—and realizing it isn't what you thought it would be.

My column was syndicated. And it turns out, the most popular ones I wrote, the ones with the most Likes, Shares, and Rts, were not the ones about my travels abroad. It was the ones I wrote about the people in town.

The Italians have a saying, *the whole world is a village.* Tutto il mondo e un paese. Hope I got that right 'cause I'm still terrible with languages. And they're right. Those stories were popular because they hit a common chord. That essentially we are all the same; human, flawed, capable of acts of heroics one minute and ones of great shame the next.

Jake played another two years with the Chicago Blackhawks. And after hoisting one more Stanley Cup above his head, which he dedicated to Mike Bresler, he announced his retirement. Since then he's devoted one hundred percent of his time to coaching kids and painting to raise money for the organization.

Kyle lives with us during the summer when he trains exclusively with Jake. If he gets any better, he's going to need an agent soon.

We were married at home on the Lake. My idea. The honeymoon in Bora Bora was his. Which is why we're back here celebrating our second anniversary.

"But what?"

Sensing my reluctance, he walks over, and grabbing my hips, pulls me closer. Close enough that our bodies line up perfectly. No fantasies necessary. Sorry, Jackie.

Dipping his head, he plants a string of kisses down my neck. "You wanna cancel and stay in."

I'd love to. Unfortunately, I married a viciously competitive man and will be branded a coward for all eternity if I do that.

"At laaaast, my true love has come along…" my phone rings, tone courtesy of Etta James.

We both glance at the screen and see Charlie's number flash.

"Better get that," Jake says, smiling.

"Jackie's going into labor!" Charlie howls the moment I hit Accept, frantic as always whenever his wife has a baby. This one counts as number three.

"Calm down, Charlie. The doctor said everything looked good. There's no need to panic."

"Zelda's here and I can't take her psychoanalyzing me right now."

"You've been mother-in-law free for the first five years of marriage. She's only trying to make up for lost time."

We've been lucky, last month marked my mother's second year in remission.

I'm not saying we take mother-daughter vacations, but things with Zelda are much better. Part of me just enjoys watching Jackie force her to change dirty diapers when we all get together for the holidays. Nan's turning 85 this year and keeps saying she's willing to live to 100 for no other reason than to keep an eye on Zelda. At least she stopped calling her a hooker. Because fair is fair.

Regardless of how any of us feel about my mother, Dad is happy and as long as he remains that way, we've vowed not to interfere.

Elvis proved himself to be the filthy scoundrel I suspected he was. Apparently he did have a few fornications left to give. He managed to escape again. Thankfully, I had nothing to do with it. One day a small white cat showed up on our doorstep, demanding to be let in. Naturally, Nan was not going to turn her away. The joke was on us when she delivered three grey, black, and white long haired monsters two months later.

I glance across the room to find Jake at the door, pointing at his empty wrist.

"I gotta go Charlie. I have a date with some sharks. Tell Jackie we'll swing by on our way back to New York."

An hour later, as I'm gazing over the edge of the dive boat into translucent green waters. A school of baby sand sharks waiting to eat me circle below. It doesn't take much to convince me that my pride isn't worth the risk.

"Honey…Sunshine…Light of my life?"

Jake stops checking his air gage, expression super intense, and meets my apologetic smile. We don't agree on everything, but we agree on the most important thing—always listen and respect each other's choices.

"Remember when we were in New Zealand, bungee jumping, and you said I could never ever get you to say mercy first?"

His brow quirks. Then he places the aluminum scuba tank on the bench and comes over to me. He leans down until we're practically nose to nose. Close enough that I can count the gentle creases at the edge of his deep blue eyes and the freckles under his coffee-with-cream tan.

Cupping my face, he kisses me. "Never ever ever, Carebear. Turners are not quitters. Now, are you a Turner or are you a Turner?"

His teammates are probably glad he retired. "I'm a Turner."

"Damn right, you are. Suit up, baby. I checked your tank and you're good to go. Promise you're gonna love it."

"Never ever?"

"Never ever," my handsome Scrooge of the Adirondacks repeats with a teasing smirk.

"I'm pregnant."

The smirk drops and his mouth parts. "Mercy."

About the Author

Paola Dangelico loves romance in all forms, pulp fiction, the NY Jets, and to while away the day at the barn (apparently she does her best thinking shoveling horse poop). She was born in Milan Italy, grew up in New Jersey watching her father paint the covers of bestselling romance authors like Danielle Steel and Amanda Quick, and after a long stint on the left coast returned to the right coast to write about finding love in a modern world. Presently, she resides in New Jersey with her fur family.

Facebook Reading Group (P. Dangelico's Mod Squad)
Facebook Page P. Dangelico Author
BookBub
Pinterest PDangelicoAuthor
Instagram PDangelicoAuthor
Twitter- @PDanAuthor

Or find me here
www.pdangelico.com

Printed in Great Britain
by Amazon